if I fail

Everfall Series Book Two

L. B. ANNE

JOA PRESS
FLORIDA

ISBN: 9798715822543

Before I Let Go, book one of the Everfall series, took us on Aria's time travel journey back to 1982 to prevent her own suicide attempt.

This installment is a new adventure, connected to the first. There are still angels watching over the students. But there is also an evil force that would prefer they destroy themselves.

***

From the end of *Before I Let Go*...

Aria was on the roof of the dormitory with Brandon. She had just talked him out of jumping. He took her hand, and then...

ONE

Ypsilanti, Michigan
November 1990

"Oh, no! Not again!"

A static-like current ran up my arm and radiated throughout my body. Bright light surrounded us.

I want to disappear. I don't want to feel my body anymore—the pain.

Were those Brandon's thoughts I heard? He was just in the middle of screaming for help at the top of his lungs.

"Whoa, chill. You're going to hyperventilate." I didn't know what was happening, but there had definitely been some kind of mistake. Let me explain why. Once upon a time there was an angel who had one job to do—convince

1

a girl she had reason to live. Done. Check it off the list. The next thing she knows—not even thirty minutes later—she's back floating in time. "I can't believe this is happening again."

"What do you mean again?" Brandon asked between deep breaths. "I'm vibrating. Are you vibrating?"

Yeah, that was part of it, and also the feeling of being nowhere and everywhere. I looked around us. "Where is the owl? I didn't see it this time."

"Why are you mumbling? Do you know what's going on?" Brandon asked.

"I-I'm not sure."

"Where are you?" he asked.

By the sound of his voice, he was about to lose it. "Aria?"

"I'm right here."

"Where?"

He can't see me? I stood directly in front of Brandon, close enough to reach out and touch him. But when I did, my hand passed through his arm. "I'm decide you."

He looked all around while grasping the sides of his head.

"Try to stay calm."

"How do you suppose I do that? I'm standing in the air, surrounded by light, and you disappeared, but I can still hear you. Then—"

Brandon stopped talking, seeing the white around us transform into swirls of color. "It's like a kaleidoscope," I thought aloud. The colors combined forming images. Different scenes faded in and out.

"Do you recognize any of that?" I asked, because I sure didn't.

He didn't respond.

Then a single image expanded out, taking up the whole area around us. It came into focus as a corridor of a school.

"I know this place," he said.

"I do too."

We waited, wondering what was going to happen next. I raised my arm to ask him about the school, not that he could see me, and my sleeve pulled back. *What is that? An owl tattoo?* I had no recollection of getting one. There was no way I had a tattoo. My father would kill me.

The snowy owl on my wrist was identical to the one that had taken me back in time. *Wait a minute.*

"Ask him," a gentle voice instructed.

"Ask him what?"

Brandon looked around. "Is there someone else here? Who are you talking to?"

Almost transparent students exited classrooms and passed through us.

He examined the backs of his hands. "I'm changing. Am I shrinking? Am I dying?"

Ask him, repeated in my head. I instantly knew what I was supposed to do but had no idea why. "Will you take the journey even though you know where it leads?" I asked.

Brandon continued looking around us, trying to find me, I think. "What does that mean?"

"It means you must go back and figure out where it started."

"Where what started? Go back where?"

In an instant, the fourteen-year-old him walked down the Stoneburg Academy hallway, and right past me. He wore the same burgundy blazer and black slacks as the rest of the students, with a backpack slung over his shoulder.

Look at him at fourteen. He's so... Awkward. Boy is he going to age well. Have a good journey, Brandon. I hope yours goes better than mine did. Well, mine ended well, but—hold on... I looked down at my school uniform and opened my blazer. *Why am I here too?*

I watched Brandon over my shoulder. He looked back, and we stared at each other for a moment. *Does he know it's me?*

My brows raised, but he turned away.

I continued down the hall until I saw a bathroom and ducked in there. A few girls rushed in laughing and went straight to the stalls, talking over the wall about a dance.

I stared at my reflection. At least I was in uniform this time. *I'm still fourteen,* I thought. But I no longer had a bald head. Tiny wisps of curls were forming. Pixie cut style. If the bangs grew longer, I could've had a nice punk rock 'do.

Why, oh why am I back here again? I whined inside. *Am I a regular time traveler now?*

The girls exited the stalls, still talking, and washed their hands.

"Are you okay?" asked the one smelling of cigarette smoke.

"Yes."

"Hurry, before the late bell rings," her friend told her, while handing her a stick of gum.

As soon as they left, I heard that gentle voice again. "It's more than you traveling through time."

I jumped. "Who said that?" I waited for a response. "You—whoever you are. You heard my thoughts?" There was no owl this time, so what was I hearing? Maybe someone was in there and heard me. But I hadn't spoken. I opened each stall door to see where the voice came from. The restroom was empty.

"This is a gift," it continued. "Your gift."

"What kind of gift?"

"To help those like you who have stopped living. Those who have become blind and can't see the blue of the sky or the green of the grass. They don't dance in the rain, make angels in the snow, or enjoy a baby's laughter. Those who have withdrawn into themselves and have given up. They are those whose very being has been taken captive."

I looked around and up at the ceiling. Was the voice in my head or was it audible? The smooth back wall caught my attention, and I examined every inch of it for a hole.

Someone could be on the other side playing a practical joke on me. "Captive? How is that possible? By what or who?" I asked.

"It once had you."

"It?"

The voice was soft, familiar. "Are you my mother?"

"No."

My heart sank for a moment. I would've loved to see my angel again. "I'm fourteen. What am I supposed to do?"

"Go outside."

"Go outside?"

A bell rang, but it wasn't the late bell. Commotion came from outside the door. I stepped into the crowd of burgundy blazers as all the students and teachers filed out of the building. The fire alarm continued to sound.

We huddled together several feet away from the school, shivering, and although I wasn't exactly bald anymore, that breeze hit my scalp like wisps of ice lashing at it.

"Look over there. What's going on?" someone to the right of me asked. Everyone in earshot strained their necks to see what was happening on the other side of the parking lot.

"Excuse me," I said as I pushed my way through the students until I could see around them. There were news vans parked along the curb and a cameraman was out there filming the school.

Just ahead of me, a hoarse voice asked, "Did you get a letter?"

"No. Letter about what?" asked Kennedy.

Jessica didn't respond. Was she talking about *the* letters? As in the letters I wrote?

I wasn't shivering anymore. Heat rose from my collar.

Someone gave the *all clear,* and the group began moving, hurrying back into the school. I stood in the center of the lobby with the crowd impatiently bumping into me while passing. If I'd known what period it was, I would've gone to my class. Instead, I went to my locker. I suddenly remembered taping a copy inside the last time I returned.

Just as I turned the corner, my eyes met those of Mrs. Kohn. It wasn't a surprise. She was often outside of her counselor's office talking with students. But on this occasion, she carried a box, and looked to be leaving. Her long bangs covered one eye. She flicked her head back, because one eyeball couldn't possibly give the results she wanted from her cold stare. It averted any thoughts I had of saying hello to her.

"Aria!" Donna stepped between us as Mrs. Kohn walked by.

"Hey! Do you know what's going on around here?" She whispered. "The police are here."

"Why?"

She looked up and down the hall, cupped her hand to the side of her mouth and whispered in my ear. "I made sure everyone received their letters."

"What does that have to do with the police?"

"Well… Now, don't split your wig."

7

"I'm not wearing a wig."

"You know what I mean."

She hesitated for a moment. "I also made copies… And mailed them to the newspaper—"

"Donna…"

"And then they printed one of them in today's paper." Her face flinched as she waited for me to yell.

I gasped. "Which one?"

Before she could respond, hands grab me and push me back against the lockers. "What did you do?"

Her hazel eyes glared at me, her brows almost connecting at the center, the way she scowled.

"Stop!" Donna said as she grabbed one of her arms.

My fingers curled into a tight fist. I was no longer the girl trudging through each day filled with fear and despair. I was back to the girl I was when I first arrived from New York, filled with strength and courage, and if it was a fight she wanted, a fight was what she was going to get.

"Let go of her," said a voice from behind her.

TWO

Kennedy spun around so fast that she backed into me, her low ponytail swinging into my eye. Her tone quickly switched up from that of an evil witch to an innocent little girl. "Brandon..."

While watching her performance, a memory surfaced of Kennedy having spent the night at my house. "Tell me a secret," she'd said as she sectioned her hair, wrapped tissue paper around her pink sponge roller, and carefully rolled a lock of hair around it.

"I don't have one."

"Yes, you do. Everyone does. Tell me something no one knows. It will seal our sister bond."

I hesitated. I'd begun to see Kennedy as a person who couldn't be trusted. Still, she was my best friend, so I told her. "I collect feathers."

"Stop making stuff up. Tell me a real secret."

9

I fluffed the curls of my ponytail as if I were actually doing something special to my hair as she went through her nightly routine. Next, she'd smear cold cream over her face for her imaginary wrinkles.

"It's true. I have a jar I'm filling."

"For real? Why do you collect feathers of all things?"

"You'll laugh."

"No, I won't. I promise." She crossed her heart, kissed her finger, and held it up to the sky.

"I like to think they're from angel wings. So if I find one, it means an angel is near. It makes me feel lucky."

"Ooh... I want to see. Where is it?" Kennedy scooted to the edge of the bed and looked around the room.

"Hidden. What about you? What's your secret?"

She moved closer to me. "There's this boy named Brandon at school. He has this long Jheri curl, and he is so dreamy."

Dreamy? She'd been watching Grease. I knew it. Even though she said she hated that movie.

"No way. You really like him, don't you?"

She blushed and yelped into the pillow she'd been squeezing on her lap.

This was the Brandon she'd mentioned. Why couldn't I have been facing her, so I could see her expression as she faced her crush? Brandon hadn't seen that side of her before, or her demeanor wouldn't have changed.

A group of kids stopped to watch what was happening. They formed an arc around us just far enough away to be out of range of a wild punch or kick.

Kennedy cleared her throat. "I was—"

"Didn't she recently save your life?" Brandon snapped.

Why couldn't she turn around so I could see her face?

"You've got it all wrong. It's not what it looks like," she replied.

"Basket case," Donna mumbled.

"Shut up," Kennedy hissed. She looked as shocked as I did when Brandon grabbed my hand and pulled me away.

The disgust in his voice was the punch to the gut that I was ready to give her. If only he'd arrived two seconds later.

We pushed through the students and stopped around the corner, near the science labs. Donna followed close, pulling her thick red hair forward, over her face, and held her head low. She did that when she didn't want anyone to notice the way her mouth twisted, making it appear oddly small, with one jaw higher than the other.

"This is private," Brandon said over his shoulder.

Donna stopped walking.

"Don't talk to her like that." She was the one person who had my back. I wasn't about to let him treat her that way. He needed to know that from the jump. "Give us a minute, Donna."

She pointed away from us with a question on her face. "I'll be right over here," she said.

"It *is* you, right?" he asked, looking at my hair. Or lack of it.

"Me who?"

I checked out his, too. His Jheri curl swept past his shoulders, but it wasn't oiling up his blazer and dripping like Uncle James's.

He glanced over at the few students rushing by and whispered, "From the future?"

"Are you crazy? What are you talking about?"

He stepped back. "Ummm… Ha! You believed me? I was just kidding with you about that future stuff."

"I was too," I said with a grin.

"You think this is funny?" His hand pointed hard at the ground. "Tell me why I am back at the one place I never wanted to see again."

I didn't think anyone could hate Stoneburg Academy as much as I did. "What happened to you here?"

"No. You first. Explain this."

"I can't."

"What are you, some kind of witch?"

"No! If I were a witch, I'd send *you* back in time. I wouldn't send myself too!"

"Then how am I back here? And why are you acting like this is no big deal?" He rubbed his hand over his stomach and lifted it away as if it were hot to the touch.

"Because I've gone through it already."

The bell rang.

"We're late. We have to get to class."

I walked away, but Brandon pulled me back. "What class? I'm not about to sit in a classroom with a bunch of kids."

I pointed at his reflection in the upper window of the lab room door. "Have you looked at yourself? You're a kid."

"I don't want to look at myself. I have a Jheri curl! And do you think I remember my schedule from what is this—six years ago?"

"1982."

"1982? Where am I supposed to go?"

"Donna," I yelled up the hall. She was still there, waiting on me, even if it meant being late to class. She leaned forward, off the wall, and looked toward me. "Meet me right here after school."

Her hand raised with a thumbs up and she hurried away.

"Come on," I told Brandon.

"Where?"

"To the office to find out where you should be."

He looked toward an exit door. "I've got to get out of here."

"That's a bad idea." I pointed outside. "News crews. Truant officers. Police. And they call your parents when you skip. Besides, maybe, together, we can figure this out."

"You have an accent here."

"I do? That's right, I did. I recently moved here from New York. I mean, back in 1982 we moved here, to

Michigan. That's what you hear. In 1990, my accent only reveals itself when I'm around other New Yorkers."

He followed me to the glass-paned double doors of the office, looking confused and a little afraid.

"Do you remember anyone in here?" I asked as we stepped up to the counter.

"Faces but no names."

His eyes searched the room and stopped on a boy. "I know that guy. That's Calvin."

Pigeon-toed Calvin. The girls loved him. Possibly the handsomest boy in the school. He did a double take, looked at Brandon and then me. He pointed. "I need to talk to you."

I turned and leaned my back against the desk.

"What's that about? Why does everyone want to talk to you?"

"I-uh..." I shrugged. It wasn't necessary that he know about what I'd gone through. Especially since he didn't seem to remember I'd been an outcast. "Were you friends?"

He tugged at his necktie. "For a while."

"Because?" I held it out, egging him to tell me more. "There she is." I leaned over the end of the counter. "Ms. Harris! Over here!" I said as I raised my hand.

She came over to us. "There *is* a line, you know?"

"I know, but we're in a hurry."

"Do you need to make a call?"

"No. He lost his schedule."

She looked confused and smirked as if we might be playing a joke on her. "You already know your classes."

"Uh, yes, but one of them moved," said Brandon.

"Good answer," I whispered, surprised how fast he came up with that.

"Okay, hold on a minute."

"Always talk to her, and never to the one with the mustache, Mrs. Wallace." Half frame reading glasses hung from a beaded chain around her neck, and she looked as if she'd never smiled a day in her life.

Ms. Harris, not much younger than Mrs. Wallace, was always jovial. "Here you go, Brandon. And here are late passes for both of you."

"She knows my name?"

I nudged him.

"I mean, thanks."

Brandon followed me out of the office and looked at his schedule. "Go up those stairs and to the left."

"You remember your way around here?"

"I told you, I've gone through this already."

"How long ago?"

"Too soon for my liking."

He looked up the stairs. "I can't do this."

"You can. Don't worry. If someone tells you you're in the wrong seat, just laugh it off and move." I pointed at the trophy display case. "I'll meet you right over there after school, okay?

"What? Why are you still standing here?"

"Slap me."

"Excuse me?"

"Slap me hard, so I wake up. We're in the same dream, so let's slap each other at the same time. That should work."

"Sure, why not?" I whacked him good.

"Oww... I wasn't serious," he exclaimed, holding the side of his face.

"Now do you believe it's real? You didn't wake up."

The sound of heels clicking over the tile floor came from around the corner. "Hurry," I said as I pushed him. "Listen, all you have to do is stand back and watch everyone else. Don't say any more than you have to, then no one will ask what's wrong with you or why don't you know or remember this or that. Let them lead the conversation. Here's my number, just in case something happens." I wrote it on the back of his class schedule.

"Something like what? What could happen?"

"I don't know."

"How do you remember your phone number?"

"My father has never changed it. Oh, and disguise your voice to sound like a girl's when you call." *That shouldn't be too hard for you,* I thought. I didn't want my dad questioning me about boys. I wasn't ready for the conversation he might decide to have. Fourteen was too old for the birds and the bees talk.

One of the office doors opened and Calvin pranced out with a huge grin. He placed an arm around Brandon as if they were best buds. "What's up, man? When did you two become such good friends?" he asked, looking back and forth at us.

"I've got to get to class," I told Brandon. "After school?"

"Yeah," he replied.

"See you around, New York. And I *will* see you. We're science partners, remember?"

"Can't wait," I threw over my shoulder.

I knew what he wanted. To know what everyone else wanted to know: Did the newspaper have a copy of the letter I wrote him? Was he next?

I looked back.

Calvin started up the stairs. "Are you coming?"

Brandon hesitated. "Yeah."

Now that I knew what period it was, I hurried to my class. I'd asked Donna which letter was in the newspaper, but I'd already figured out it was the one I'd written to Mrs. Kohn.

I glimpsed a boy a few seats over, trying to put away a copy of the paper without the teacher seeing.

"Psst, can I see that?"

He held it low so the teacher wouldn't notice and passed it to the girl beside him. She handed it to me.

I held the cover of my textbook open with the paper inside. I skimmed down through the paragraphs of outrage from the reporter, down to my letter.

I remembered and recited every word in my head, line upon line, without really reading. Why had I written to her? I never believed she would read it or understand. I pictured her wadding up the paper and slam dunking it into the trash can. Still, I wanted her to know how I felt about her and her actions—the effects they had on students. My letter meant I was here—I am here. And even if you don't think so, I mean something.

Mrs. Kohn,
You humiliated me. A student never expects to be harassed by her counselor. You helped break me to a point where I thought I couldn't be fixed. Do you know what you should've done instead? Your job. You should have been my mentor. I'm at an impressionable age. Stoneburg is a college preparatory school. You should have guided me academically. And you should have offered suggestions for my social development. But you put your niece and her issues above what was right and came after me because of the lies she told you. An adult, coming after a kid. You don't deserve your position. You play a role in something much bigger that is happening at Stoneburg. My mom has always said, what you do in the dark will come to the light. A day will come when everyone will find out what you're doing.

I exhaled heavily, and the girl beside me glanced over. I handed the paper back.

"Crazy, right?" she whispered. Her name was Tracey. She'd never spoken to me before. At least I didn't remember having a conversation with her before. "They suspended her," she added with a nod.

So that's what happened. I wasn't unhappy about it but wondered what it meant for Kennedy and her crew.

I didn't have to wait to find out.

THREE

I joined the students filing into the hall to get to their next class. The clomp of loafers rushed up behind me. Then it was the "move" and "get out of the way" that made it clear they were heading for me.

"Aria! Wait up!"

I quickened my pace.

She ran to catch up and grasped my shoulder. "I know you heard me."

I stopped and looked at her hand. She removed it, and I faced her.

"How many letters are there?" asked Denise.

I scratched my nose. "I don't know. How many do you want there to be?"

"Don't play with me," said Jessica, pressing between the other girls to stand beside Denise.

One of the girls pulled her back. "Watch it. Teachers are manning the halls today."

"Play with you, hunh? Yeah, I forgot how much you and your friends like to play games. Here's a riddle for you. There is a one-story house where everything is red. The walls are red, the doors are red. All the furniture and bed are red. What color are the stairs?"

"Red, of course," Denise replied.

"Aaa!" That was my buzzer sound. "Get back to me when you figure it out."

They continued discussing it as I walked away. "Didn't she say everything was red?"

"Let's ask Mrs. Connelly," one of them suggested.

"Then will you tell us?" Denise yelled up the hall.

I'll just wait for the big bathroom confrontation. That's your MO.

"There you are!" Donna exclaimed after school as I approached the hall near the main door.

Two boys smiled into our faces as if giving a concert, rapping the chorus of Grandmaster Flash and the Furious Five's "The Message" as they dance-walked around us. One of them put on a Kangol hat, so he looked the part. I guess it was okay to wear a hat in school now that everyone was going home.

"Hey, hey, hey. Too much noise. Take that outside," said one of the teachers.

"Donna, you're about to lose your scrunchie."

She grabbed the end of her ponytail. "Oh."

"I have something to tell you."

21

She stopped moving, and the kids behind her objected loudly to her halting like that. "What is it? That boy. He's your boyfriend, hunh? Well. I'm kind of…"

"What?"

"Never mind," she replied.

I pushed her out of the hall traffic path. "I think you would've known about it if he were my boyfriend."

"Are you sure?" She gazed at the ceiling as if she were having a daydream about her own life. "It could be some kind of secret love, like in a movie."

"Earth to Donna." I snapped my fingers in front of her face.

"Then what is it?"

"It's going to sound unbelievable."

"I'm already used to unimaginable things with you."

"Well, brace yourself… I went to the future and came back to 1982."

She fell back against the lockers as if someone had pushed her. "You did not! Today?"

"Right before the fire drill. Do you believe me?"

"I almost peed myself just now. What is happening? Of course, I believe you. Haven't I always? I mean mostly?"

I pursed my lips.

"Okay, give me a little credit. I believed you quicker than anyone else would. So, what happened?" she asked, excited.

"Things were different in the future. Coming back here the first time changed things."

"Like what?"

"Like we were best friends."

"We already are."

"But we weren't before I came back here. And we're roommates in college."

Her eyes brightened. "Really? I'm in college with you?"

"Yes." I looked around for Brandon while realizing it may not be okay to tell Donna about how things were in the future.

"Oh, he left already."

"Who?"

"Your boyfriend—the boy you were talking to earlier. I saw him with Calvin."

"Why did he leave?"

"I don't know. Because school is over?" she said with a smirk.

"Smart aleck. Okay, well, I'll catch up with him later. But brace yourself for what I'm about to tell you."

"As long as you're okay with missing your bus."

I popped myself on the head. "How did I forget about that? Walk this way."

She hurried alongside me. "Keep talking. I want to know everything."

"He's back too."

"Who's back?"

"Brandon."

"That boy? I know you're not saying… From the future?"

I nodded.

Her eyes were wide. "Is that what he was so anxious to talk to you about? What the heck is going on in the future? Or what's going on right now that's bringing you guys back? I know *you* had to come back to reclaim life the first time."

I liked the way she put that. On my last journey, I reclaimed my life by choosing against suicide.

"Yeah... I don't know Brandon's story, but I'm going to find out. Bye!"

"Wait! Am I weird there—in the future? "

"Weird how?"

"How do I look?"

"Oh, you're beautiful!" I yelled as I ran backward.

Never had Donna had a bigger grin than at that moment. I mean, as big as her mouth would allow due to the malformation. "Call me!" she yelled.

I ran toward the school busses. Some of them were already pulling off.

The cold air whipped around me, blew my skirt back, and focused on my knobby knees. I stood outside the door of my bus staring at the grooves of the black steps and then toward the corner store across the street. The city bus stop was right past it.

"Are you getting on?" asked the driver.

I wasn't sure. Had I been riding it? I shivered and pulled my hat down over my ears. It was too cold to wait for the city bus, but I was tempted to, so I could get away from students. How can you think things out on a noisy bus?

A boy approached. Jacob from my street. He ran past me and up the stairs. I followed him on and found a seat near the middle of the bus. There were a few familiar faces behind me. Especially the ones who watched me. I turned forward, not sure what to expect. School bus rides could be the worst. If you're being picked on, you're trapped there until their stop or yours.

When the bus pulled up to the end of my street, I hurried to get off and power walked home, leaving Denise and Jacob (the only other kids to get off at my stop) behind as if I were winning a hundred-meter dash.

The screen door on the side of the house was unlocked, and the door was open. "Dad!" I yelled down into the basement and then ran up the three stairs into the kitchen. He stood from the table. "Why are you yelling? What's wrong?"

I didn't answer. Instead, I laid my head against his chest and hugged him tight.

He squeezed me. "Hey you. What's happened?"

"Nothing. I'm happy to see you. Plus, you're warm."

"And *you're* freezing."

"Do we have coffee?" I walked over to the coffeepot. "Ooo... You made some," I said as I took a cup from the cabinet.

"Since when do you drink coffee?"

That's right, I'm fourteen. "I was testing you," I said with a laugh and put the cup back.

"The last thing I need is you bopping around here on caffeine, pop-locking all over the place."

"I didn't-I mean, I don't do that, Dad."

"Only because I don't let you drink coffee."

Debarge's "I Like It" played softly on the radio. I swayed a little to the falsetto chorus.

"See, that's what I mean."

My father was more serious than my mom. She would've danced with me. I grabbed his hands and moved side to side. "Come on, Dad."

He took two steps and dropped his hands. "That's all I've got." But those two steps meant the world to me because he tried.

"Dad, did anyone call me?"

"Who, you?"

"Yeah, me."

"No, Donna has not called, but I'm sure she will—about twenty times. You're still shivering. How about some tea?"

"That'll work." I hurried to my room, rubbing my defrosting fingers. I picked up the receiver of the phone and held it between my shoulder and the side of my head as I dialed zero.

"Operator…"

"Can you give me the number for Brandon… Brandon…" *What in the world is his last name?* "In Stoneburg…"

"I'm sorry, but I will need a last name."

"Never mind, thanks." I hung up. I'd have to wait for him to call me.

The tea kettle whistled. *That was quick.*

"Aria, all we've got is Lipton."

I hurried to the kitchen. "That's all we ever have."

"Maybe you should wear pants with your uniform and stop rolling your socks down like that in the winter. I know you have leg warmers. I've seen them. At least you're wearing sneakers instead of those jelly shoes."

"I'm wearing pants tomorrow.

"I wish it would snow, though," I said as I looked out the kitchen window.

He stepped behind me and placed his hands on my shoulders. "Your mother loved snow. Not the cold weather, but she could sit at the window for hours watching the snow fall." His hands dropped, and he walked away. I had to remind myself that although my mom's passing was years ago for me, it was only weeks ago for him.

"How about a game of chess?"

"*You* want to play chess?"

"Yes, I'll set up the board." I hated the game, but I knew it would create a happier mood for him.

"All right. As long as you don't mind getting whooped."

"I think you mean me putting a whooping on you," I said with a laugh.

My father was no fool and hugged me unexpectedly. He knew what I was trying to do. And as I melted in his embrace, I glanced out the dining room window. An enormous shadow passed over the backyard, too large and close to be an airplane.

"What's wrong?"

He felt my body stiffen and looked out the window.

"Is something out there?"

"I-I don't know."

FOUR

I couldn't explain what I'd seen outside. But it gave me chills. By the size of the shadow that lingered over our yard, it was huge.

My dad went to the window. "I don't see anything out there."

"That's weird. I thought I saw—I guess it was my imagination."

"Well, think about how bad I'm going to whip you in this chess game. That won't be your imagination," he replied with a chuckle.

After being thoroughly humiliated at chess, I spent the evening on my best school-girl behavior, completing all of my homework assignments on a Friday night instead of waiting until Sunday.

Thank goodness I had a diary to help me get caught up on things. As I held it, I had a recollection of telling myself to write what took place each day in case I ever needed to remember something.

Okay, what have we got here? I stood from my beanbag as I read. *My class assignments each day, what I ate each day, what I did each evening. It's so detailed. Did I have a premonition I'd return?* A few pages back, the words around the bottom half of the page were surrounded by stars forming a rectangle. *I guess this is important.* I read the bullet points. "This is how you get to school on the city bus. This is where your school bus stop is. This is where the spare key to the house is hidden. This is where their secret clubhouse is. I don't know what else to call it." *A clubhouse? Like the Mickey Mouse Club?* I almost laughed. *Why would I write that?* There was a blank line next to it. *Why hadn't I filled in the location?*

I switched on my radio and laid back on my bed singing the J. Geils Band's "Centerfold" while holding the journal above my face. Something hit my window. I sat up. Another one. *Was that hail?* I got on my knees and looked outside. *Who is that?*

I pushed up the window. "What are you doing here?" I whispered.

"Come out. I need to talk to you."

"You could've called me. Why didn't you wait for me after school? And how did you know where I live?"

"The phone directory."

"But there are probably a hundred Meyers in there."

"One hundred fifty-seven. But only one with your phone number."

"This could've been my father's bedroom. Are you nuts?"

"Not with the music blasting and posters of Bernard King, Grease, and Diana Ross on the wall."

I looked back over my shoulder, thinking I heard my dad. When I looked outside again, Brandon was being yanked away. *Oh no!*

I paced back and forth in my room. It wasn't a problem that he came over, but why would he have come to my window. I needed a good excuse. *Think, Aria.*

The doorbell rang.

Why would my father ring the doorbell? Did he lock himself out?

I hurried to the living room. *I didn't tell him to come to my window. He did that of his own volition. So I'm not guilty of anything.* I took in a deep breath and pulled the front door open.

"Uncle James?"

"Look at this joker I found snooping around." He spoke loudly on purpose, trying to blast that he'd done a good thing to whoever was in listening range. He held Brandon by the collar of his jacket as though he were holding up a puppy.

"What's going on?" my dad asked, coming up from the basement.

Uncle James let go of Brandon. "Stalker," he accused as he unzipped his snorkel parka.

"No. I was trying to make sure I had the right house." He held his hand out as my dad walked into the room. His voice shook. "Mr. Meyer, I'm Brandon. Aria and I have a school project. I just wanted the notes I missed."

The old school project excuse. Amateur.

"Project?" He turned to me.

"Yeah, come in. I've got the notes. I'll get them. Dad, relax. It's about school. Seriously." It wasn't a lie. His visit may not have had anything to do with a school project, but it was definitely about school.

"I've never heard you mention a Brandon before."

"He's a boy who is my friend. My friends in New York were always boys. This is nothing new."

"Yeah, but you weren't fourteen with hormones."

"Whatever that means."

Both my dad and Uncle James gave Brandon the evil eye as he skirted past them. My father never held his tongue. He said what he wanted to say in front of people, whether they liked it or not. That's why everyone trusted him. They knew he would always be honest.

I grabbed my backpack from the kitchen chair. "Come on, Brandon," I said, directing him downstairs.

Across from the laundry room was our family room. Beyond the seating area was an additional dining area and a guest bedroom. "Dad, you can come too, if you like," I said from the stairs.

"I trust you. You hear that, Brandon? I trust *her*. I will be right here if you need me. So don't try anything."

Brandon frowned with a what's-with-him look.

"He's got nice hair though," I heard Uncle James say from the kitchen.

Brandon watched me look up the stairs to make sure my dad hadn't changed his mind and followed us. The overhead light flickered before releasing a steady beam over the table. I led him to a chair.

He started talking, but I held a finger to my lips and turned on the radio. Thomas Dolby's "She Blinded Me with Silence" blared.

"Aria, turn that down," my dad screeched.

I turned the knob, lowering it some, and walked back to Brandon. "How did your day go?"

"I got snagged up in conversations a little, but I made it through. My family was weird."

"It was nice to see them younger though, right?"

"I guess so, but I feel like someone is playing the worst trick on us."

"Yep, been there done that." I placed a sheet of paper on the table I'd doodled over. At the top were both of our names, the year 1990, and a line drawn down to 1982. "We attend the same college, here," I said as I tapped the tip of my pen on 1990. "And we attend the same high school, here. What are the odds?"

"I thought about that too."

"Now we need to fill in these tick marks in between to figure out if there are any similarities about this year for us. We're linked somehow. We've come back in time together."

"Is that what happened?" he joked. "I don't want to be back in time. Do you know what kind of childhood I had? No one wants to come back to Stoneburg Academy."

"No, I don't know, but you can tell me. I hated it too. What was your experience at Stoneburg?"

He looked away. "Were you skipped up a couple of grades?"

"Hunh?"

"You look twelve. Has anyone told you that?"

"I've heard it a million times. Answer the question." I was eager to hear what he'd gone through.

"You have a really strong voice for such a little person. You're kind of tough too. I wouldn't imagine you had any issues at all at Stoneburg."

"Brandon, stop analyzing me."

"I'm telling you what I've noticed, comparing us—trying to figure it out."

"No, you're avoiding my question."

"Everyone was talking about a letter at school today. Did you hear about it?"

"A letter? Yeah. So this is what I think is happening..." I changed the subject because I didn't want to explain that I had written the letters, why, and what I had almost done to myself. "Something happened to you at this age. At

Stoneburg. In ninth grade. Now, you don't have to tell me what it was, but it had to be severe."

Brandon didn't respond in words, but his expression told me a lot. "So what about it? I mean, if something happened, why would I have to come back?"

"To go through it again, differently. We all have bad experiences we have to deal with. We are supposed to grow from them and not let those things defeat us. The first time, you did something terrible—I'm guessing. This is your chance to make it right. Like to heal yourself, in a way."

"Heal. Interesting choice of words. But I don't understand."

I sighed and stared at the books I placed on the table to make it look like I was trying to find the notes for him. "I came back because the first time, I committed suicide."

"You were resuscitated. That's what your speech in class was about, right?"

"Yeah, that's what happened the first time, but I changed my past when I came back."

"And you left out the time travel part."

"Yeah, and you can understand why."

"But now you are back here with me. Is it different from the last time?"

"It is. I kind of had a guide. And I believe I'm supposed to be that for you."

"A guide, hunh? What did it do?"

"It mostly asked a question."

"What question?"

"The same one I asked you. 'Will you take the journey even though you know where it leads?'"

"It asked you that?"

"Will you take the journey even though you know where it leads?" I repeated. "All the time." I focused on the dark back wall of the fireplace across from us. "There's something else..."

"Well, what is it?"

"You only have so much time or..."

"Or what?"

Maybe I shouldn't tell him. But isn't he going to find out anyway? Or was it only after me? "Well... This thing that doesn't want you to succeed will interfere. It doesn't want you to save your life or have a future."

He sat with his elbows on the table, chin resting on his clasped hands. "Now I'm in some horror film. Is this the Twilight Zone? What is it?"

"I don't know. I've only heard it. But I can tell you that you never want to hear what evil sounds like. I was really depressed at the time...

"It preys on those who have withdrawn into themselves and have given up. They are those who have been taken captive—by-by..."

"By what?"

"The Murk." *The Murk?* My eyes bulged from their sockets. The Murk. I knew what I meant. That thing that tried to torment me under the church. I still hadn't told anyone about it. But it had a name, and I somehow knew it.

Brandon sort of laughed. "Sounds like the monster or villain of some movie. That's it! I appeared in the wrong movie!"

"Not funny. But you don't have to be afraid."

"I'm not."

"Yes, you are. That's why you're cracking jokes. Look, you need to focus. The sooner you remember what happened to you, the sooner we can finish this journey."

"I'm trying to, but only bits and pieces are coming to me. But that thing you mentioned, h-how will it—I mean, will it appear out of nowhere? Like in your bedroom while you're sleeping, or while you're taking a shower and it just appears and grabs you?"

"Again, this isn't a movie. But you'll hear it before you see it, planting fear and negative thoughts in your head."

"You're kidding, right? I thought it was going to bust up in the room, exploding through the wall or something."

"I'm not kidding," I said with a straight face.

"Then how did you get away when it came after you?"

"This owl flew in and—"

Brandon snickered and leaned back in his chair. "Did you say an owl?"

I nodded. "Really an angel."

"What? Where? You're trying to say—but..." He kept starting sentences and stopping.

"I know. I know." I lowered my voice. "Something happened to me, and I'm wondering if something similar happened to you." *You can tell me. Just tell me already!*

He looked at me oddly and pointed. "You. You're that girl."

"What girl?"

"I remember. Oh, wow."

"What?"

The floor creaked above, and seconds later Uncle James bounded down the stairs to the basement.

"Yeah, that's what we're going to do. Just follow that part," I said as I handed some papers to Brandon.

"Got it." he said.

Uncle James wore a black silk shirt and green bell-bottomed pants. He stood in the doorway with a hand on his hip and the other stuffing the end of a Twinkie into his mouth. "Done?"

"Yep."

"Brandon, my man. You want to ride? Let's go and get tacos. It's a Friday night and there's nothing to do but—"

"Uncle James!"

"That's right, you're kids."

"Tacos from where?" asked Brandon.

"Taco Bell. It's just around the corner."

"Sure."

"Get your coat. You too, Riri," Uncle James said as he jogged up the stairs. "You can tell me all about this school project on the way."

I turned to Brandon. "They have Taco Bell in 1982?"

"Yeah. You didn't know that?"

"Nope."

"Your family didn't eat out?"

"Rarely. My mom's food was too good."

"The tacos are like thirty cents."

"Stop playing."

"I'm serious."

"You need to get out more, Riri."

"Hey, only my family calls me that."

"Not anymore."

Uncle James was already heading out the side door. We followed him to his car. "Word to the wise. Cover your nose and mouth with your scarf while you're inside his car. He uses too many of those tree air fresheners."

But Uncle James had something new to display. He'd purchased tiny bottles of musk scents from a convenience store. "What you know about that, Girl? You don't know nothing about that," he touted.

The scents were even worse than the tree air fresheners.

I looked in the backseat at Brandon holding his scarf over his nose.

Uncle James glanced in his rear-view mirror. "Do your parents know where you are, boy?"

"Yes, sir," Brandon coughed.

As we drove, I looked up at the night sky. It was brighter than usual, as if a lamp was lit behind the clouds. I studied the neighborhood. Things always looked different at night;

all the stores lit up with lights made it seem we were somewhere else. In 1990, many of the restaurants remodeled to updated versions and some stores I remembered were closed or replaced. *There's Fashion Bug, and Wendy's is still there. And over there should be...* I did a double take. The front of a plaza suddenly blacked out. Then it appeared again. I jumped and blinked hard. Was I seeing things?

"Girl, what's wrong with you?" asked Uncle James.

"Charlie horse. I'm okay," I said as I rubbed my leg, still eyeing the window.

Uncle James turned up the radio and did his best James Brown imitation. Normally, I'd laugh. But I looked back at Brandon. His eyes asked what was wrong. I motioned my head toward the window. The leather of his seat squealed as he shifted to look outside, but I didn't think he saw the dark shadow that kept pace with the car. If we stopped at a red light, it stopped, and even shifted to the other side of the street.

Uncle James pulled into the lot beside the restaurant and parked. It was like magic, the way his hair pick appeared. He used the rearview mirror to watch himself pick out his curl, sprayed curl activator on it, and picked it again. "I have to keep it fresh for the ladies," he explained. "You guys coming in?"

"Yes," said Brandon.

"No. We'll wait."

"Are you sure?"

"Yes, it's cold out there."

"All right then. Don't get upset if you don't get what you want. Thirty crunchy tacos it is," he said as he shut the car door.

Brandon quickly sat forward. "What happened?"

I got on my knees facing the back seat while looking out the rear window. "You know that thing I told you about."

"The Murk, right?"

"It's following us. At least I think that's what I saw." And possibly what was outside my kitchen window earlier.

"But I looked. I didn't see anything."

"I don't think you're supposed to."

I bit my lip as I looked around.

"You're making this up—trying to scare me into remembering."

"No, I'm not."

"You have to be. There's no such thing. If there were— What was that?" He turned, looking to the right of the car. "Did you see that?"

FIVE

Brandon grabbed the door handle to open the car door. I pulled at him. "Get back in here. Push down the lock. You don't know what's out there."

"What's happening?"

Everything went black around us. We couldn't see the parking lot, the restaurant, the road, or each other. I opened Uncle James's glove compartment searching for a flashlight and found one. Shining the light through all the windows did nothing to help. We couldn't see anything through the blackness.

"Where did everything go? What is happening?" asked Brandon.

The car shook. Brandon grabbed hold of my seat. My right hand held the flashlight. My left hand clasped his.

If he looked out the windshield, I looked out the rearview window. If I looked out the driver's side windows, he looked out the passenger side. It was like we communicated without having to—both set on catching a glimpse of whatever had blocked our view and not allow it to sneak up on us.

"This is what I warned you about." My voice was almost a whisper.

"That Murk thing? What does it want?"

Not willing to let go of Brandon's hand, I dropped the flashlight and reached for the steering wheel. If I blew the horn, Uncle James or someone would come out and save us.

Before I could grasp the wheel, the car lifted on one side and I fell back into the passenger door. Brandon fell away from my seat. I tried to remember everything that happened before when it came for me. My guide was there, flying alongside me as I ran, and then it fought to save me so I could get away. Was that what I was supposed to do? Open the door and face this thing by myself?

"Aria, I feel something happening!" Brandon yelled. "It's pulling me!"

"How?" I was looking right at him. "Don't let go," I heard in my head. That gentle voice. I looked at my hand. I'd been holding on to Brandon the entire time until then. My angel didn't let me go. I righted myself, slipped between the front seats and grabbed hold of Brandon's arms. You would've thought a tornado surrounded us the way we thrashed about. That thing was mad.

Then I remembered it stopped when I accepted my journey.

"Brandon, will you take the journey even though you know where it leads?" I screamed.

The car lifted in the air and slammed to the ground. I rocked back, hitting my head on the dash. I lunged at him again and held tight.

"What happened to you?" I screamed.

"What does it want?"

"You!"

The darkness subsided. We were both panting. Brandon held to my arms for dear life. My chest heaved. "Whatever you became after whatever happened to you, it wants you there in that place. The you that was going to hurl himself off the dormitory roof."

Everything went still outside. "I think we're safe." I released him, and he let go of me. We both fell back into our seats. The cars to the left of us and the dumpster behind the building came into view. "It's gone," I whispered. We relaxed and sat in silence. A few minutes passed, and I rolled down my window to air out the car for a moment and rolled it back up. One of us may have farted while we were freaking out.

"Definitely the Twilight Zone," Brandon murmured.

The driver's side car door opened, and I nearly jumped out of my skin.

"Here ya go, Riri." Uncle James handed me a huge bag. I was so happy to see him. The car filled with the scent of taco meat and corn tortillas.

He glanced over at me and then back at Brandon. "What's the deal? Did I scare you or something? Good googly moogly."

"No. I'm okay. We saw a rat."

"You guys are way too scary for high schoolers.

"How about this," he said as he shook the bag. "I've got enough tacos here to feed the entire block. Those bubbas in there thought I was joking when I told them how many I wanted." He laughed. "They weren't happy, but that's their job, right? Now go ahead and tell me about your project," Uncle James said as he started the car.

I think Brandon was too freaked out to say anything. I was too, but one of us needed to act normal. "Uh, we're working in groups. We have to support whether we believe time travel is possible or not."

Brandon tapped my arm and pointed. Donna sat inside the restaurant in one of the booths, across from a boy. He looked familiar. He had that whole David-Hasselhoff-*Knight-Rider*-show hair thing going. *I'd rather have Kitt, the Pontiac Trans-Am he drives.* Maybe he was her cousin. She'd tell me later.

"Traveling to the future?" asked Uncle James.

"Or to the past."

"Good googly goop! Uncle James has the answer for you!"

"You do?"

"Time travel is possible, but the problem is there being two of you. If you go to the future, there's two of you. If you go to the past, there's two of you."

I glanced back at Brandon. He had a valid point. We were going back in time, occupying the original us. This was something totally different. As if I didn't already know.

"You guys have Kool-Aid at the house?"

"That's the one thing we always have."

"What flavor?"

"Grape."

"Sounds like a party," said Uncle James.

Despite having the scare of our lives, Brandon ate about ten tacos. Maybe he was a nervous eater. And I don't know if it was because I was younger and my taste buds were different, but tacos in 1982 tasted so much better than they did in 1990.

After we'd eaten and played a few video games—we mostly stared at the television screen—Brandon said he needed to get going. My dad asked if he wanted a ride home, but he said he would walk. I followed him outside. "You're not afraid to walk home after what happened?"

"You mean death trying to take me? No," he lied. I could tell. He wouldn't look me in the eye. "I have to face whatever is happening, right?"

"Are you sure? We can give you a ride."

"It's okay."

He looked up the street as Uncle James came out of the house. "Leaving, Riri." He hugged me from the side and walked toward Brandon. "Boy, get in the car. I'll drop you off."

"I hate to tell you, but he's not going to take no for an answer."

"I can tell. Oh, and you're pretty cool."

"Aren't I?" I joked and nudged him.

"Thanks for not letting go."

How did he know about that?

"Let's go, Brandon," yelled Uncle James.

"Don't worry, his crazy is harmless."

"If you say so, Riri."

"Don't call me that."

"Good googly goop!" He said with a chuckled as he walked to the car. I knew I'd never hear the end of him joking about the way Uncle James spoke.

I watched the car pull away. They both waved, Brandon while holding his scarf over his nose.

I closed my eyes as wind blew over me. The cold air felt different from the air in New York. Cleaner. I opened my eyes, realizing I was beginning to feel as if I'd just moved to Michigan. I was losing the future feeling already, settling into my fourteen-year-old self. That wasn't good. *But I didn't let go*, I thought to myself and grinned. I was pretty proud of how I fought to hold on to Brandon.

"You're going to fail."

I spun around. I felt a chill that did not come from the cold wind blowing at me.

"His path is set. You cannot change it. He already made his choice," the voice groaned.

I froze there, ready to run, but not sure if I could. It was near, I could feel it and feared it would attack me.

Headlights flicked on from down the block. A car approached, blinding me for a moment. Whoever it was, had their bright beams on, and switched them to low, seemingly to get my attention.

The car came to a stop in front of my driveway. "I don't know what you think you're doing, but you've stepped out of line. Stoneburg is *my* school. Do you hear me? There's nothing you can do to change that."

What was she doing on my street—at my house?

"Doesn't matter what happens. I'll be back. Look out for yourself."

Mrs. Kohn sped away, and I backed up into my driveway. She didn't just randomly drive through my neighborhood. She'd been waiting—watching. If I didn't know better, I'd say she was sent by the Murk.

SIX

There was something about mornings. They washed away the events of the night and made everything like new or like bad things that happened were only a dream. I awoke, opening one eye, staring at my Cabbage Patch dolls at the end of the bed and hurried to the bathroom.

I screamed.

"What's wrong?" my Dad yelled from the other side of the door.

"You left the seat up again."

"My bad."

"I almost fell in!"

"Stop walking to the toilet with your eyes closed."

He knew me so well. I barely looked where I was going all the way into the bathroom. It was a miracle I'd even fallen asleep after how agitated I was.

Mrs. Kohn and the Murk haunted my dreams. She swayed back and forth in a cemetery with her back to me.

And they were working together to stop me from doing something. But since I awoke, I couldn't remember what that was.

My dad looked up from his newspaper as I walked past and into the kitchen. I wasn't just hungry, but hangry as he would say. That's when you're so hungry that your stomach is angry about it and growls super loud to let everyone know. It may even cramp up like it's going to fold in and eat itself.

I was fully awake now and bounced along in my purple plaid flannel pajamas and sweat socks, humming The Clash's "Rock the Casbah," the last song I heard on the radio the night before. I took a jug of milk from the refrigerator, set it on the counter, and grabbed a box of cereal. My dad was quiet, and I could see him watching me.

"Hunh?" I asked as if he'd called me.

He rubbed the sides of his face with both hands. A newspaper lay on the table in front of him.

He tapped his pointer finger on the newspaper.

Oh boy.

The newspaper was only a couple of steps away, but those two steps may as well have been a hundred feet.

I leaned over my dad and read. I didn't gasp, but I'm sure my eyes did. The Stoneburg Journal printed the letter I wrote to Dean Richards. Two letters in two days. Because of the evening I'd had with Brandon—too many tacos, crazy Uncle James, and oh yeah, a run-in with the Murk and its minion, Mrs. Kohn—I'd totally forgotten about the letters.

Dean Richards,

I've tried not to blame you. You can't be everywhere. You're a nice man, but I wish you knew about all the things that were going on right in front of your face. It's *your* school. Your counselors harass us like they are part of a clique of kids. No one is making sure we are safe. You do your job and go home. Open your eyes. We're being bullied, robbed, and beaten. I didn't just shave my hair off because of my mom's cancer, but because of what I was dealing with, and it all took place at *your* school. You are failing your students. Wake up. Something is happening at Stoneburg and you need to stop it before it gets worse.

I gulped. The whole school would now know who wrote the letters. I'm the only kid who shaved her head and whose mom had cancer. I could see Mrs. Kohn laughing her head off that I was now exposed. I felt weak all of a sudden and wobbled. My dad steadied me. "Hey, sit down."

I slid into the chair beside him.

"The first letter I wondered about. But this one is clearly from you." He pulled the letter I'd written him from beneath the paper and read it aloud. I didn't want to hear it or be reminded of it. It was a hard time, but I wasn't hurting anymore like I was when I wrote that letter.

"Dad,

I'm sorry I was so angry with you. What went on with you and Mama was between the two of you. But I felt like you broke up our family and broke Mama's heart. You broke mine when you left, only because I really needed you. It's hard to be a student and a daughter and a nurse when you're fourteen. And I was dealing with so much. I needed hugs and encouragement. Not that things would've been any easier. I just needed you. I forgive you."

"I'm sorry."

"Don't apologize for this. Apologize for leaving the refrigerator door open and causing our food to spoil. Not for this. You did a good thing," he said as he stood and closed it.

Is this a trick?

"You were hurting, and you wrote letters. You didn't have malicious intent. You wanted the pain to stop."

My shoulders relaxed.

"I wish you would have told me it was that bad at Stoneburg." He pointed at the paper. "Is all of that still going on?"

"I don't know, so put your shotgun away."

"I haven't pulled it out yet. You know I will go up to that school and show them who's the what."

My eyes teared hearing him use Mama's favorite phrase. He realized it, grinned, and lightly touched the side of my face.

"It's better. At least for me."

"I'm proud of you," he said and hugged me.

"But… It's in the paper."

"Because you sent it to them."

No, Donna did.

"Isn't this what you wanted? I think it's a good thing. Besides, no one knows you wrote it."

I rubbed over my barely-there curls.

"Oh, well, that part *would* give it away. But no one is going to say anything. You'll get strange looks, but that's it. All eyes are on your school right now. If anything goes down, you get out of there and get to a pay phone, and I'm on my way."

He was about to get riled up. I placed my hand on his shoulder to keep him from standing. All I could do was walk to the counter and pour Fruit Loops into a bowl, trying to act as if I wasn't worried anymore.

This was too much excitement for a Saturday morning. Students that were fond of Mrs. Kohn now knew I caused her suspension. Everyone: teachers, counselors, janitors, office staff, the dean… they all knew the girl who shaved her head and whose mother died.

My dad tugged on his robe that hung open around me and draped over the floor. I'd taken it from the hook on the back of the bathroom door. "I would like to wear this sometimes, you know? It's so big it's swallowing you whole."

"Yours is so much warmer than mine. When you shop, why don't you buy two of everything?" I suggested with a chuckle.

"Can you imagine the fit your mother would have if I had you around here dressing like me?"

We both laughed and fell silent. At that moment, I realized how much my father missed her too. Even if they were getting a divorce.

The phone rang. I reached around the cabinet where it was mounted on the wall. "I've got it, Dad. Hello?"

"I saw it!"

"Donna?"

"I mean hello." She always sounded as if she were holding something in her mouth when she spoke. "But I saw it. I'm so sorry. If I hadn't sent the letters to the paper, no one would know you wrote them. It's all my fault. Why did I do that? I was only trying to help. Me and my big ideas. I'm so sorry."

"Donna, Donna..." I put the phone down at my side and brought it back up to my eat. She was still apologizing.

"Donna!"

"Yes?"

"Stop beating yourself up. It was bound to come out some time."

"What are we going to do? Do you think they will print them all?"

"I don't know. Did you read them?"

Her voice dropped. "I tried not to, but I couldn't help myself. I'm sorry."

"Then you know what's in Kennedy's?"

"They think they have problems now, wait until they read that one."

SEVEN

"Aria!" Jonas exclaimed as he hopped out of my grandmother's orange Chevy Chevette. I loved that car as much as the Dukes of Hazzard car I was saving up for. It was the car that all the kids at school talked and daydreamed about receiving with a big red bow on top, during their sweet sixteen birthday party.

I ran up the drive and hugged my little uncle. No one else's family that I knew of had the age differences that my family had. I picked up my uncle off the ground and squeezed him in a bear hug. How many kids could say that?

"Aria, put him down. Let me get in there."

I hugged her too. "Hi Grandma." The sight of her made me wonder if she'd been in a rush. She hadn't even combed out her curls. She must have awoken, pulled the rollers out of her hair, and hopped right in the car for the three-hour drive.

"What are you doing out in the cold without a coat on, Aria? Let's get inside. At least you're not barefoot this time. You look better," she said while walking toward the house.

Movement caught my eye, and I saw Denise's living room curtain fall back in place. *Nosy. I bet she's watching me so she can report if she sees any news reporters or anything. Or she has her little brother doing her dirty work and reporting back to her with his findings.*

"Dad, someone's here to see you!"

"Who—Ma, what are you doing here?" He was as happy as a little kid to see her. It amused me to witness this child-like side of him. He rocked her back and forth as he hugged her, as if they were dancing. "Get over here," he playfully told Jonas, kissed him hard on the cheek, and hugged him.

Jonas wiped his jaw off.

I took the shopping bag my grandmother carried and set it on the table. I didn't expect it to be so heavy and almost dropped it.

"Be careful, hear?"

My grandmother was so funny to me. She said "hear," after everything. "You go and pick that up, hear? Don't pour all that applesauce on your porkchop, hear?"

As I watched them chattering away, I wondered the same thing as my dad. What *was* she doing in Stoneburg?

Everyone knew my grandma didn't like highways. It usually took an emergency for her to drive long distances. My thought was since my mom's passing, and I didn't choose to live with *her*, she wanted to check on me. She also could've come to make sure my dad was doing okay and cook him a few of his favorite meals for us to freeze. She did that, but if I were reading or playing with Jonas, I'd look up and she'd glance away. If I were chopping onions or peppers for her, she didn't watch to make sure I was careful with the knife. She eyed my face instead of my hands.

"I can see you watching me."

"I'm glad to see your hair is growing back, that's all. What on earth got into you?"

"Come on, Grandma, you know why I shaved it off."

"Yes, because of your mom. God rest her soul. Mmm hmmm…" I could tell she knew it was more than that.

"Booga booga booga," I exclaimed as I dropped the knife and dashed after Jonas with my veggie-soaked hands reaching for him. He squealed with delight.

"Stop running. Come here, you two, hear?"

I guess the conversation wasn't over.

"There's something different about you."

"Different good or different bad?"

"Good." She brought her face close to mine. Close enough for me to see her few moles, which looked like freckles over her cheeks. Our noses almost touched. A grin formed on her face as she looked into my eyes. "There it is. You're glowing."

"I've been using cocoa butter like Mama—"

"No." She backed away and shook her head. "That's not what I meant."

"I'm happy?"

"You are, praise God, but that's not it. Jonathan, are you going to get me that perch, so I can fry it up?"

"Yes, ma'am," my dad responded from the basement. I heard him close the freezer, grab his car keys, and hurry up to the door.

"I think you're out of cornmeal too."

"That's because Aria makes hot water cornbread almost every single day."

"Hey, don't complain. You eat it too when you're home. I'm usually hungry after school," I explained. "It's one of the few dishes that I've mastered, besides French fries."

My dad poked his head in the kitchen and made a face at me. After he shut the door, the lock clicked, and the car started, Grandma stood and looked out the window. She watched my dad move her car and then pull his car out of the drive. Then she turned on the television for Jonas, sat him in front of the Underdog cartoon, and walked back to the kitchen table where I sat.

"I'm going to tell you something that's going to be extremely hard to understand, hear? But I think, deep inside, you already know?"

My brows raised as I waited for her to finish. She asked a question, but I didn't have an answer for her. "Know what?"

"That you have a special gift."

She knows? She couldn't. "What kind of gift?"

"An ability that no one would ever understand."

I looked away. I couldn't tell her. She would think I was crazy. I would think I was crazy. I didn't even know why Donna believed me. "I—"

She cut me off. "I don't need you to tell me anything about it."

"You don't?"

She scooted her chair closer. "It runs in the family. It's a gift. But with it comes a responsibility. And each gift is different. Understand?

"No."

"You'll grow into it."

Grow into it? She had no idea what I was dealing with. "What exactly is it that runs in the family?"

She leaned back over her chair, looking into the living room at Jonas, and quickly leaned forward. "You're a gleamer," she whispered.

"Ha! Grandma, stop playing. I know you're making this up."

"I know I have a reputation of telling stories. Yes, I tell them to keep people entertained at parties or gatherings. They're funny exaggerations, but this is not one of my stories."

"Grandma, I didn't know anything about your stories. But a gleamer?"

"Yes, you have a calling to help people. It won't be easy, and there is much you must learn, but it will take some time. I suppose you have some concerns or questions?"

Do I have questions, Grandma? I have tons of questions. Where do you want me to start? I'm really in college but I've come back in time to 1982 and can't leave until something happens or I help someone, neither of which I know what I'm supposed to do anything about. But that wasn't a question. Concerns? Oh, yeah. That too. There's something out there trying to get me. And oh, I almost forgot, my school is from the pit of hell.

A pot boiled over on the stove, and Grandma leapt from her seat.

"Mama once told me if you put a wooden spoon over the top, that won't happen."

She smiled at me, and I took the moment she was busy with the pot to run in and play with Jonas.

The doorbell rang.

I looked through the peephole of the front door and then out the front window but didn't see anyone. Then I ran to the side door.

"Hey."

"Do you know what a phone is? Come in. I was going to call you anyway to see if you figured anything out, but we have company."

"Who's this?" asked Grandma while drying her hands on a dishcloth.

"Brandon, this is my grandmother."

He waved. "Nice to meet you."

"Is this..." Her brows raised.

He looked at me and back at her. "No, no, no. No, ma'am. It's not like that. We have a school project."

There he goes again with the school project excuse.

"We're going to go downstairs."

"It was nice to meet you, Brandon," Grandma yelled after us, as he followed me to the basement.

He looked at the wall across from the sofa. "Is that a real fireplace?"

"No. The logs are fake. You can put your coat right there on that chair. Sit down. Are you okay after last night? Have you figured it out?"

"That was… I don't know what that was. I had to sleep with the light on—once I actually slept. Random memories are coming back to me."

"Yeah? Anything we can use to figure out what's going on and get us back to 1990—preferably before Monday? I don't want to endure another Stoneburg school day.

"I'm with you. There are bits of things, and feelings. So much pain. And uh…"

"What?"

He wouldn't look at me. "Things I'm ashamed of…"

"We all have those kinds of things. No one does everything right. Just this morning I—"

Brandon looked at me as if he'd just recognized me. "Did you write that letter?"

I rubbed over the bandana I'd tied over my head. "I'm not the only girl at the school with short hair."

"Yes, you are. Everyone else has big hair, relaxers, perms, or braids. And..." he stared at me a moment. His eyes lowered. "Your mom passed. I'm sorry."

"It's okay."

"No, I'm really sorry. Oh wow, I just remembered when I found out. I need to go. I know why it's coming for me now."

"Why?"

"Because of something I did—what I was a part of."

"But—"

He grabbed his coat and ran up the stairs. "I'll see you at school."

"Brandon, you're not staying for dinner?" Grandma yelled.

"No, ma'am. I have to go. It was nice to meet you."

The screened door closed behind him. Jonas ran up to us and looked up at me, his big brown eyes brimming with too much concern for a kid. "He needs help."

I picked him up and tickled him. "What do you know about it?"

After Brandon left, I'd planned to ask my grandmother about the Murk. If she knew I had a gift, and I was this gleamer thing, she could have the answers I needed. But with my dad back from the store, Jonas, and all the fun we were having, I never got the opportunity, nor thought about it again.

"It's time to go, Jonas," my grandma said later that evening. He hid under the table and wouldn't budge, but she pulled him out.

Grandma zipped Jonas's coat. He protested by unzipping it and taking his arms back out. She'd put it back on him and he'd take it off again. "Stop it. We have to go, Jonas. If we hurry, we'll get back in time for Bingo."

"It will be too late for Bingo. Stay the night," said my dad.

"I wish I could, but we need to get home. We'll come back soon.

"What's that outside in the driveway."

I looked out the window, thinking she saw the Murk.

"A car," my dad said.

"Look at theat. You have a car too. You can come and visit us, hear?"

"Use that Sulfur 8 hair oil I left you, hear? It will make your hair grow back faster."

"She will."

"Dad, no," I whispered. "It stinks like rotten eggs."

"I know. Just say okay."

"Will do, Grandma."

She hugged me tight. "If you don't let go, you won't fail," she whispered in my ear.

My mouth dropped, and she looked in my eyes as if saying, *you know exactly what I'm talking about.*

After we said our goodbyes, thank you for the food, and I smothered Jonas in plenty of kisses and hugs, I was free to think about what both Grandma and Brandon had said. He knew why the Murk was after him, but did that mean he knew why we were back here? And I couldn't begin to think how my grandmother knew to use those words.

"Aria," my dad called. "Are your clothes ready for church in the morning?"

"Church, really? You go?" *Since when?*

"It was your idea. Oh, I know what you're doing. Ah, ah, don't try to back out now."

"I'm not. I mean, I'm glad we're going."

"Okay, well go ahead and iron your clothes, and get to bed. Don't stay up late on the phone with Donna."

I stood there with an *I'm grown* look and then remembered that I wasn't. I guess it was time for bed. "Good night."

EIGHT

"We're going the wrong way, Dad."

"No, we're not."

He pulled into the parking lot of Denise's church. The one she'd invited me to attend youth night at with her. But it was only so Kennedy's goons could chase me afterward.

"This-this isn't our church."

My dad stepped on the brake, and I jerked forward. "What are you talking about? You're the one who suggested we start attending this church."

"Yeah, I like this church. I was kidding," I said, trying to cover myself.

"Heh, Riri, I don't know about you sometimes."

"It's because I'm a teen. We're kind of wishy-washy."

"I guess so," he replied, looking more concerned than amused.

If we were attending this Denise's church now, we could run into her family. And if they'd read the paper…

I removed the thought from my mind. At least I didn't have to sit with her. I remembered the message from youth night. "Beware of sweeping your faith under a rug while you're at school, becoming a different person. And pulling it from beneath the rug when you get home." That was Denise's way of life. She sat in church and listened to these sermons. Then I guess it dissolved from her brain.

"Are you okay?" asked my dad.

"Yes…"

"Does that mean you're getting out of the car?"

I realized I was sitting there in a daze with my hand on the door handle. "Uh, I was trying to remember last week's sermon." *I'm such a bad liar.*

We arrived late and sat at the back of the church. Ushers tried to take us to the front, but my dad objected with the wave of a hand. He wore his best black suit, and I wore the same dress I'd worn to my mom's funeral. One of the few I owned. I completed the brown ensemble with white tights. They were textured and thick like wool socks. It was too cold for stockings.

A baby on the pew in front of me wouldn't stop watching me. I crossed my eyes at her and then filled my cheeks with air. My dad tapped my arm, and I exhaled the air from my ballooned jaws. The choir sang a hymn I didn't know. As I took a hymn book from the holder on the back of the pew in front of me and listened to them sing, I thought of Brandon.

I didn't know about anyone else, but I could always figure things out in church. It was the only place where my thoughts—instead of being jumbled all over the plate—lined up, and I had a keen sense of being alive and everything working out. That feeling often stayed with me the entire day.

My dad nudged me. "You need to drink more water. Your lips are dried out," he whispered and handed me lip balm.

I turned away, only slightly embarrassed. My lips always chapped in the winter. As I bit my lip, I peeled back a thin patch of skin. I don't know why I got such joy out of doing that. It was gross, I knew. And I rarely used lip balm. I pulled the piece of skin from the tip of my tongue and looked at it. At least I didn't chew it up and swallow it like I did as a kid. The skin reminded me of the glue I let dry over my finger and peeled off when I was in elementary school.

I stuck the lip-skin inside the program a greeter had handed us when we walked into the sanctuary. Instead of it being used to tell us the order of the service, it was a skin holder. I almost laughed and suddenly realized that's what I need to do—peel off the layers. Get to know Brandon. Then, without him telling me, maybe I could figure out what happened to him.

A few pews ahead of us, a little afro bobbed around on a thin neck. The back of Denise's head was next to him. Her Jheri curl was pinned up in back, and a few loose ringlets hung on her neck. As far as I knew, they were in church every Sunday, often the first family there, and she sang in the youth choir. I shook my head. What a charade.

The pastor said the benediction, signaling church was over, and we and walked out into the lobby.

"Hey, Mr. Meyer. Aria, can I talk to you for a moment?" Denise smiled so charmingly I almost thought I'd gone back in time to when she was a sweet person—the person I first met when I moved to Michigan.

I sauntered over to her.

"Kennedy wanted me to talk to you."

"At church?"

"She says you stole her boyfriend."

"Again, we're in church and I don't have a boyfriend."

"That's what she's telling everyone—among other things."

"Why are you even talking to me? Let me guess, we have a truce on Sundays?"

"I'm trying to do the right thing and let you know they're planning something. Don't say I didn't warn you."

"Consider me warned," I said as I began to walk away. "Unlike the night you set me up."

"You need to watch out," she added with attitude.

I gritted my teeth. *Don't do it Aria, don't do it. You're at church.* I turned back to her. "Do you believe God sees and hears everything you say and do?"

"Yes…"

"No, you don't." I left it at that. Something for her to think about. She didn't say anything further.

I walked over to my Dad wearing a huge fake grin.

"Ready?" he asked.

I nodded just as Denise's mom approached. "Mrs. Matthews!"

"Jonathan, I keep telling you to call me Dorothy."

"Habit. I wondered if Denise would like to come over and join us for Sunday dinner."

My head and Denise's snapped toward him.

"No," I whispered. "No, Dad."

"It's been too long since the girls spent any time together."

"Dad, what are you doing? I don't want her to," I whispered. "That's *our* time to spend together."

"It's okay with me," said Mrs. Matthews. *Of course she said yes. She figures my mom recently passed, so I need the female company. Great.*

Denise looked dumbfounded. I was with her on that.

"What do you say, Denise?" asked my Dad.

"Sure, I mean that's fine, I guess."

Dad, you just invited the devil into our home, I screamed in my head.

"We'll see you in about an hour?"

Denise nodded.

My dad grinned as if he'd done the most amazingly thoughtful thing.

Our parents walked ahead of us to the parking lot.

"Now we're supposed to pretend we like each other?"

"Why does your father want me to come over?" she whispered.

"I have no idea. You could've said no."

" *You* could've said no."

"We're not even friends. I never even asked you to be my friend."

"No. Your father did."

NINE

"He did what?"

"Yeah, before you arrived from New York, your father asked me to be your friend. He said you wouldn't know anybody, and he wanted you to like it here."

"Is this what you call being a friend?"

"Look, I warned you. I told you the kids at Stoneburg may act like they like you at first, then they turn on you."

"You told me to watch my back. But you didn't tell me it was a warning about you too."

"I'm not as bad as you think."

"Yes, you are. You're biding your time. Until what, I don't know."

Her mouth dropped open. She was going to say something but seemed to decide against it. "Bye, Traitor," she said instead as she walked to her car.

"See ya later, Sewer Sludge." That was the worse I could come up with while still on church grounds.

"This is going to be nice; don't you think? Spending the afternoon with someone other than me."

"I like spending the afternoon with you, Dad. We have fun. When you have a weekend off, we don't have to spend it with other people."

"I appreciate that, but there's nothing wrong with you spending time with females."

"I don't need females. I need family. You don't care about me hanging out with females. This is because of Brandon, isn't it? He's a friend, no different than Donna."

"This is not about that boy. Go and change, I'll start reheating one of these meals your grandma made."

I sulked all the way to my room, trying to figure out how I could get out of dinner. My options were to fake a stomachache, cut or disconnect the wires to the doorbell and then pretend I didn't hear anyone knocking, or nail planks to her doors so she couldn't get out.

The doorbell rang exactly an hour later—before I could come up with a good excuse to cancel dinner.

I watched her through the peephole, facing the road. She'd changed clothes too. I opened the door and stared at her.

"Well, are you going to let me in?"

"My dad changed his mind."

"Really?"

"Denise, come on in," my dad said, walking up behind me.

She handed him a bottle of soda. "My mom told me never to go to someone's dinner without bringing something."

"At least *she* has manners," I said under my breath.

"Wow, I haven't been in here since before your mom…" Her tone softened. "I mean, I remember how we all used to sit around the living room and talk. Those were the best days."

The door pushed open as I was closing it.

"Aria!"

"Oops. Sorry, I didn't see you, Toya."

"Denise invited me. Is that okay?"

"Of course." *Thank goodness.* "Keep her away from me," I whispered. Toya lived on our street too. I didn't see her much because she didn't go to private school like us. Our school got out later in the day than hers, and we always had a mountain of homework, so we didn't have much time to hang out. There was a time when we called ourselves the three Musketeers. That seemed like years ago instead of months. Everything was great those first two weeks in Stoneburg and then slowly went downhill.

"You girls set the table," my dad instructed, and went to the record player to choose an album. Maybe music would keep us from having to talk to each other.

Denise reached for the plates I was holding. "I don't like you," I told her as I handed them over.

"As I've always said, gotta love that honesty."

"You guys stop it," Toya whispered as she grabbed four glasses. She set them on the table and went to the freezer for ice. "No fighting," she said as she banged our ice tray on the counter, trying to loosen the cubes. "We're going to make the best of this and have fun like the old days."

"It's not like you to be vindictive," said Denise.

"Vindictive this," I said as I threw a saucer at her throat. Okay, it was only a thought, but I was two seconds away from actually doing it.

She sat at the table, and I made sure I took a seat on the opposite side, so I wouldn't end up next to her.

My dad said grace, and I hoped it wouldn't be one of his long reserved-for-holidays prayers.

"Please bless the hands that prepared it as well as the hands that provided it," he said as I looked around at everyone with their eyes closed. I refused to close mine. Denise might slip something in my drink.

We all ate in silence, as my dad went about his usual routine of dumping condiments over most of his meal. By the time he'd gotten his food the way he liked, we were a third of the way finished.

"Aren't you guys going to talk about anything?"

I shook my head.

Denise seemed to study the dimples in the peas on her plate.

"Uh, it's a nice day out," said Toya.

"Yeah, it's nice," we repeated.

My dad took a bite of his meatloaf and started choking. "What is this?" He was turning red.

"Hot sauce. Does it taste spoiled or something?"

He gulped down his water and ran to the sink to get more. "I thought it was ketchup," he gasped.

"Dad, it's a totally different bottle!" I snickered.

Denise and Toya tried not to laugh, but soon we were all howling. Our cackles broke through the thick veil of uneasiness in the room.

As much as I didn't like Denise, it was good to see her laugh. Her dimples only showed when she laughed, and I always admired them.

"That was fun," she said before she left.

"See?" said Toya.

"Yeah, but at school…"

"What?" I asked.

"Nothing. I'll see you there."

"You don't have to be like them, you know."

"I wouldn't worry about me. I'd worry about what was in yesterday's paper," she said and walked out the door.

I'd forgotten. Everyone knew it was me. And that night, no matter how much my dad tried to reassure me it would be okay. I didn't believe it.

Neither me nor my dad was prepared for what happened Monday morning. We were heading out together, him teasing me as usual. We stepped outside the front door and came to a dead stop on the porch. My smile turned to shock.

Lights flashed in our eyes. I put my hand up, shielding my face.

"Mr. Meyer," said a reporter. "Is it true that you put your daughter up to writing those letters about Stoneburg Academy?"

"Is it true you have mental health problems?" asked another.

"Is it true you tried to jump out of a window while holding your infant daughter after coming back from Vietnam?"

I gasped as my father stepped in front of me. Kennedy was the only person I'd told, other than my second grade class. I read my report and mentioned he'd been a paratrooper in the army.

Out in the street, a car crept by. I could see it passing behind the vans. She nodded toward me with a sneer. Mrs. Kohn.

TEN

"Get off my property!" my father yelled at the reporters. He pushed me behind him. His arm was like steel. I couldn't have pushed it away if I wanted to. "Get back inside."

My eyes were wild. He held my face with both hands and lowered his head to mine. "This is not your fault." His breath sprayed in my face, smelling of coffee and bacon. For a moment, I thought I was dreaming.

"I want Mama." I wanted her to come walking down the hall out of her bedroom and say, "Do you know how much I love you Aria Eden Meyer?" She would make everything better.

"Riri, you know that's impossible," my dad replied softly.

"I want my mother," I cried.

"Shh… Shh…" he said against my forehead as he held me.

Now all my neighbors knew I'd written the letters too. The whole city. And they knew where I lived. Everyone.

My dad left me staring at the front door and went to the phone. He called the police, the Stoneburg Journal, and the local news. While I still stood there. Listening. In shock.

He didn't allow me to go to school that day and he was the only one allowed to answer the phone, which rang off the hook.

A few hours later, there was a bang at the door, and I feared my father would open it and hurl whomever it was across the room and into a wall like the Hulk. But it was Uncle James. There were no 'good goobly goops' or 'good googa moogas' from him. Probably for the first time in his life, he was silent. He hugged me, and then hid the shotgun, so my dad wouldn't go threatening anyone with it.

Donna may have called. Brandon may have too, but my father didn't let me know about it. I didn't know what he or his attorney told the news, but later that evening, one by one, the cars and vans disappeared.

The next morning, when I peeked out the window, the coast was clear. My dad walked out onto the porch and down to the sidewalk in his t-shirt and slacks. I guess he was still 38-hot, as he would say, and didn't feel the winter air. He looked in both directions, up and down the block. In case the reporters had left our property but were still on the street.

"They're gone, Riri," he said with relief.

For twenty-four hours, I hadn't worried about getting back to 1990 or Brandon. I was too busy being mortified to think about anything else. I'd changed the past by writing those letters. All of this was new and not a memory.

"You don't have to go to school today."

"The way they overload us with homework, if I don't go, I'll never get caught up before exams. I'll be fine."

"Then I'm driving you. That way I can also make sure those reporters aren't camping out at the school. I don't want to have to knock the snot—"

"Dad, not the snot." I laughed. "Please don't knock the snot out of anyone today."

Normally he would've laughed too. "I've already spoken with Dean Richards and your principal, Mr. Jeffries, that joker."

"Good. I'll be fine then."

As my dad pulled up in front of the school, I watched students bundled up in their coats, mittens, and earmuffs, holding books to their chest or wearing overloaded backpacks, rushing to the double doors of the main entrance. I felt a sense of impending doom. Something was coming. I frowned, wondering if it was a memory trying to surface. Maybe it was the giant dark cloud that seemed to hover over the campus. There wasn't another cloud anywhere else in the sky.

"Are you okay? What are you looking at?"

"Nothing. Just the sky."

"Don't worry about me, Dad. I'm a Meyer," I replied with a fake grin.

He hugged me. "That's right, you are. They can't break a Meyer."

I closed the car door and waved goodbye, knowing he wouldn't pull off until I was inside the building. He'd sit there and watch, waiting for the opportunity to become the mama bear whose cub had been messed with. So he could rip someone apart.

I waved again and disappeared into the herd of students. With my hood on, no one would know who I was right away. I kept my head down and spoke under my breath, "'Because you have made the Lord, who is my refuge, even the Most High, your dwelling place, no evil shall befall you...'"

It was the first scripture I ever learned on my own. I needed the words to become a part of me. Then they wouldn't be just simple words. They would give me peace in the middle of whatever the day would bring. After all, God had my back, right?

Once I got to my locker, I noticed the looks and the whispers. I had prepared myself for it. Well, I mostly prayed about it. I didn't look around at anyone in class, but when a girl two rows ahead looked back at me, I whispered, "What are you staring at?" She didn't respond and quickly turned around.

A newspaper didn't have to tell me the city was torn between if I'd been lying or if something was really happening at Stoneburg. But anyone attending Stoneburg Academy had to know the truth. I know someone had to have seen something.

"We need to talk," said Kennedy, after second period. She'd been waiting near my locker. "I mean, can we talk?"

"I guess."

"How was your weekend?"

"Is that supposed to be funny? Did you tell her we hung out?" I asked Denise, who stood behind her.

Kennedy looked shocked. I guess Denise had spared her that bit of information. "Denise," she said.

"Our parents made us," Denise replied.

Kennedy held up her letter. "You can have this back." She snatched it back down and pushed in into her pocket, seeing Dean Richards approach. He seemed to be paying special attention to everyone.

"Is everything okay, Aria?"

"Yes," I replied.

Kennedy smiled at him, innocently. She lowered her voice. "Are you trying to get everyone fired or suspended? Or kicked out of school? Don't you care about people? No one believes you anymore, anyway."

"Do *you*?"

"I just need you to tell me…" she lowered her voice to where I could barely hear her. "Is this letter going in the paper?"

"Your guess is as good as mine."

"What is that supposed to mean?"

I whispered in her ear and walked away.

"What did she say?" asked Denise.

"Nothing."

"I got one too."

"What does yours say?"

"I don't want to talk about it."

"Well, you need to. And you need to fix this."

"Me?" Denise asked.

I looked back. Nothing had changed with these girls. Having those letters printed in the paper may have exposed me, but they would expose them too. That's why I'd whispered, "It's not over." Because it wasn't. And for a moment, I hoped every single letter would be displayed for the world to see. Although they were trying to destroy my credibility, I knew, soon enough, they'd slip up and show everyone my letters weren't a lie.

As I proceeded down the hall, a boy who sat at my lunch table, Daniel, pointed at me in passing. "You're my hero."

Then there was another kid who said, "You're so brave." And another said, "I'm so glad you said something." But they were all whispering when they told me, and none of them said anything in front of other students.

I sat at my desk in the science lab looking through the microscope. I didn't want to acknowledge anyone else or my lab partner when he walked in. If I looked engrossed in the lesson, maybe he wouldn't bother me. Mr. Hampton didn't like us talking when he talked, so it wasn't likely he'd get to say anything until after class and even then, he wouldn't, around other people, because he would be ashamed of what they might hear. But he arrived early for once and didn't care about how focused I was.

"I'm super geeked," Calvin announced as he pranced in and slapped another student on the bottom. "Things are about to get back to normal around here."

He threw his tie over his shoulder. "You look nice today, Arethra. Get it? Rhymes with Urethra, as in urine."

A stink joke. Great.

The girls at the table behind us laughed. They probably had a crush on him like every other girl in ninth grade.

"But I must say, you look nice today, New York."

A compliment after and insult? I had tied a burgundy ribbon around my head that morning, matching my school blazer. I thought I looked cute. "Thanks."

I glanced over at him and caught him doing the same to me as he sat on his stool.

He leaned sideways toward me, and I leaned toward the cabinet of beakers and test tubes to the left of me.

"Everything has gotten out of hand around here."

"You think? You guys have the media thinking my father is a lunatic. I know you have something to do with that."

He lowered his voice. "Yeah, but not directly me. What was it—the Vietnam War? It kind of messed your father up, hunh? How does it feel to have *your* dirt come out? Did you have a good day yesterday? It sure looked like it on the news."

"Calvin, would you like to take over this lesson?" asked our science teacher.

"No, sir."

He wrote on my paper. "I'll see you later. You know where."

I had no idea where, and there was no way I would meet him anywhere. I wrote "Not going to happen" on the paper, folded it, and placed it in the pocket of his school blazer.

"We'll see about that," was his response.

My second run-in with Kennedy for the day took place in the girls' gym locker room.

I walked in. willing the day to go by faster. The less time I had to spend at school, the better. I could hear their commotion before I even entered. Jessica's shrill of a laugh filled the room. I stood with my back against the end of the row of lockers.

Someone was being teased. And I mean their words were like stabbing her with a knife over and over. But I didn't hear a voice respond to any of the insults.

I stepped into the aisle behind their victim. The girl sat on a bench between the lockers, staring at the floor while Jessica stood over her. She looked so helpless. I was surprised. Though I didn't remember her name, I knew she was one of their buddies.

"Look who's here," said Jessica.

I'd planned to walk right past them, minding my own business since they were harassing one of their own. But no one deserved to be attacked like that. "So she's on a scholarship. So what? You guys think it's cool to punk the girl because she's on welfare?"

"That's what I said. Why would you do that?" Kennedy asked the other girls. She didn't realize I saw her wink or that I heard what she said while I was on the other side of the lockers. She put her hand on my shoulder, and I knocked it off.

"You're not even in this gym class. I heard you say she's on food stamps because she gets free lunch. I get free lunch. Is that a problem? I'm not on food stamps. I don't even know what they look like, but if I did, that would be *my* business. My family doesn't have a ton of money like some of you whose parents work in the shop."

You could always tell the kids of the parents who worked in the auto factories (the shop). They had the latest clothes and sneakers, went to beauty salons to get their hair done, and always had money to buy the food items that weren't included with free lunch. Namely ice cream sandwiches and sodas.

"You don't have to be ashamed," I told the girl. "Whether you're getting it free or paying for it, it's still the same food." Those were the same words I suddenly remembered my mom telling *me*.

"She's like the defender of the poor and maimed," Jessica said with a huff. "Like, oh my gosh," she said with a valley girl accent as she turned to Kennedy. That sent the girls around her in throes of laughter. Some of them were already dressed in their white t-shirts and black shorts. Others only started to change out of their uniform.

They left her there on the bench, tears in her eyes, making sure they knocked into her back in passing. With each hit, it became harder for her to hold it together. She leaned almost to her knees. She sucked in air, but she didn't cry.

"Don't worry about them," I told her as I opened my locker. "Whatever you did to get on their bad side will eventually blow over. What's your name again?" my voice trailed off as I stared inside my locker with my hands on my hips.

"Lisa," she replied and gasped.

"Kennedy," I said. That's why she was in the locker room instead of at her class.

"Is that nail polish?"

"Yep." I sighed. "They wanted it to look like blood."

"It's all over everything."

"Thank goodness my books weren't in there."

I closed the door and leaned back against the lockers. *I thought this was Brandon's journey, but here I am back here dealing with this again.*

"You're petite, but look. I have an extra set of gym clothes," said Lisa, reaching inside her locker and holding up shorts and a t-shirt.

"Thanks."

We changed and walked into the gym together. Teams were already set up for volleyball.

Kennedy was nowhere to be found. Jessica laughed and pointed, knowing I'd seen what they'd done.

"You're late, girls," said our gym teacher. She added Lisa to the team on the other side of the net and me to Jessica's team.

Jessica was the player to the left of me. Libero position. If she'd kept her focus on defense, we wouldn't have been losing the game. But she kept running into me when she went after the ball. One hard bump sent me sliding across the floor. I leapt to my feet, and our teammates jumped between us before it could turn into a fight.

When it was my turn to serve, Jessica started up again with her mouth. "She looks like a bald-headed eagle— wearing a ribbon," she chuckled.

I don't know what happened, but I tossed that volleyball in the air, slapped it, and instead of going over the net, it hit Jessica square in the back of the head. Hard. That was my plan in the first place, but I didn't know it would go off so well.

She screamed out and held her head. When she turned to me, I saw nothing but rage.

"Oops," I exclaimed.

She stared me down.

Well? my expression asked. I was ready for whatever was coming next.

"It was an accident. Serve again." the teacher yelled while walking over from the sideline.

ELEVEN

The day was half over, and I hadn't heard any of my classmates whispering around about another letter being printed in the paper. Maybe that part of this nightmare was finally over. Kennedy and her friends could chill now.

Donna and I were in the lunch line. I was eyeing the French fries while she was going on and on about the colorful paper flags all over the cafeteria and the fact that the school was celebrating foods from other countries, but for France, we had French fries. "It's so embarrassing," she was saying when I heard Jessica. I didn't know what was wrong with that girl. Her mouth was always yapping away about something—someone's teeth, someone's clothes, someone's shoes—any reason to jeer. We moved down the line with our trays.

"Chocolate milk," I told the lunch lady.

"Get away from me," Jessica exclaimed. I looked around Donna to see what was happening.

Lisa steadied her tray, trying to keep her items from falling off, humiliated again, looking like a lost puppy. Kennedy crossed her legs and watched it all play out, but I was certain she told Jessica to push her away. Everyone in the cafeteria watched her, but no one would do anything.

"Lisa," I called and pointed at my table. She was reluctant to come at first, as if someone was going to get her for doing so. "It's okay. You can eat with us."

"Go on," said Jessica, as if she needed her permission.

She sat between me and Donna.

Daniel, across from us, reached over to shake her hand. "Hi! Welcome to the misfit table." I wanted to tell him to swallow, because for some reason, there was always saliva at the corners of his mouth when he spoke.

"Hi," she replied, barely audible.

"I'm too smart." He pointed at me. "She won't play by their rules..."

Donna pointed at her mouth. "Need I say anything more?"

"N-no. Of course not," said Lisa. "I wouldn't ask about that."

"Chill," I said. "Don't be weird about it. She doesn't like it."

"And thanks to her friendship with Aria here, she's come out of her shell and is all 'I am woman, hear me roar,'" said Daniel.

Donna threw a French fry at him.

The rest of those at our table welcomed her. We had become our own little crew of outcasts. But our numbers were growing by the day.

Lisa glanced over at Kennedy's table.

"Don't worry about them."

"But everyone likes her. She rules the school."

"The only person who likes Kennedy is Kennedy. Everyone else fakes it."

She didn't touch her food and sat writhing her hands together in her lap.

"Does this happen to you? Check this out. When I haven't eaten and I drink something, I can feel the liquid glide down my throat and run all the way to my stomach." I ran my hand from my neck to my stomach as I said it.

She laughed at me. "No one can feel that."

"I can. Then I feel it flow into my small intestine."

"Now you've gone too far," said Daniel. We all laughed and ate our lunch, and for a little while, Lisa's mind wasn't on her harassers.

Though no one said it, I knew they were all swallowing and waiting to see what they felt.

Lisa was quiet, but at least she ate in peace. I worried what would happen to her when I wasn't around. I wasn't told this, but it's the way I saw it play out in my head. I'd been their victim, so I knew their method of operation. When they had her off by herself, maybe on the way home from school, they would get back at her—like tigers following an injured gazelle. Or they'd wait for her in the bathroom and rough her up like they did me. Or lure her out somewhere where there were no witnesses.

"Donna, have you seen Brandon?"

"Nope." She looked around the cafeteria. "Is this his lunch period?"

"No."

"I think so."

I hadn't told her about the Murk or what happened when we were in the car that night. I was a little troubled that I hadn't seen him—okay, maybe a lot. But I fixed my face and even acted like I was on the top of the world—a big step from the day before when I felt I was on the bottom. If I worried, everyone would worry. Lisa about what Kennedy might do to her, Donna about me, and those at the table, that things weren't really changing for us peons.

In my next class, students whispered about a letter. My ears perked. They said there was none printed. I gave a whole cheerleader cheer inside my head. My drama was over. Now I could totally focus on Brandon.

But my excitement was short lived. I overheard the worst news of the day. Mrs. Kohn was coming back to work.

"Nuh-uh."

"She is. I work in the office," the girl said. "They say the investigation is over and she'll be back next week."

How could that be? She made the board of directors think I lied. That was the only answer, and probably the reason the other letters weren't being printed.

Before the end of the day, I was called to Dean Richard's office. Although Mrs. Wallace frowned at me, Ms. Harris looked up as I walked in, with the concern of a parent. "You can go right in, Aria."

"Dean Richards..." I said from the doorway.

"Yes, Aria, come in."

I sat, and he stood and walked behind me and closed the door. I didn't like him being behind me. He could choke me or something for writing the letter. "The school is under investigation," he said as he walked back to his desk.

I didn't know what he expected me to say. I stared at his tie. Then I remembered my mom saying you should always look a person in the eye, or it appears you're lying.

"I must say, I'm shocked by everything that's happening. If you were indeed being bullied, you should have come to me."

If?

"But... I want to be sure you know that I respect your decision to take this public. I mean, your parents. If everything happened as you say it did... I'm sorry, I meant your father's decision." He cleared his throat. "To quote you, 'Something is happening at Stoneburg and you need to stop it before it gets worse.' Can you explain what you meant by that?"

I tried to remember what I'd meant, not that I would tell him. I knew it was true, but I didn't have a recollection of what the information was. "I don't remember."

"But you wrote this," he said, holding up his letter.

I glanced at the letter and then down at my fingers in my lap.

"Aria, I've been interviewing students all day."

My brows raised and then relaxed. *What students? I didn't see anyone leave my classes.*

"Is there anything you would like to share with me? If someone has been bullying you, I need you to tell me who it is."

I looked him in the eye. "It's too late for that."

"No, Aria. It's never too late. Is anyone bullying you?" He leaned forward and said each word slowly, as if I didn't speak English and wouldn't understand if he spoke quickly.

"No, sir."

"Are you sure?"

"Yes."

He sat for a moment in silence, watching me. I don't know what he thought that would accomplish. It wouldn't make me come up with something more.

"May I go back to class?"

"Yes, and my door is always open for anything you want to talk about."

I hurried out. The eyes of everyone in the office were on me as I trudged through.

The bell rang, signaling the end of the day, as I stepped into the hall. Students rushed out of the classrooms—most scampering to get to their lockers and then to their busses. I pushed through them and headed to the end of the long corridor near the gym. It led to an exit door where the creative types hung out: Musicians, drama, art. Boys were usually there after school with boomboxes break dancing or hung out doing whatever else it was they did down there. The whole snare drumline of the marching band was in that hall practicing too, because the band room was on that side of the building next to the backstage rooms of the theatre.

I walked up listening to the boys, laughing and cracking jokes on each other. They didn't notice me. I knew names from my classes but hadn't really interacted with most of them. I heard Brandon's name and looked around the group for him.

"You're so bald I can see your brains," said Yankee. I never knew if that was his real name or a nickname.

"I know you're not talking with teeth as big as your eyes," this kid Carl told him.

"I know you're not talking. Your Jheri curl is so dry it's making me thirsty," said the one biting into a chocolate bar.

"At least my pants aren't sucking me down to my socks, Muffin Top."

All the boys fell into each other laughing. The one with the chocolate bar stopped chewing and rolled his eyes. That's when I noticed Brandon. He'd been right in front of me, but from the back I didn't know it was him.

"Brandon?"

"Aria."

"Are you okay?" I asked.

"Yeah." He walked me away from them where he wouldn't have to yell over the music, and no one would hear our conversation.

"I haven't seen you all day. You look so different. What happened?" I touched the bald spot on the back right of his head. He pushed my hand away and pulled on his hat. "I couldn't do the whole Jheri curl thing. I used my father's clippers to cut it off and then I lined it up." He touched his head. "But when I went to go over this section again, I forgot to put the guide back on. I cut a bald spot in my fade and had to come to school like this. My father wouldn't let me stay home. Are parents really that naïve to think we won't get clowned about it?"

"No, I think they feel we can take it. Or that it may even be good for us to deal with—unless this is his form of punishment for you."

"I don't know how it happened. I've got skills with clippers and always cut my own hair when I don't have time or can't afford to go to the barber."

"The 1990 you has skills. Not the 1982 you."

"Then I should remember how."

"I told you, the longer you're here, the more you start to forget about the future."

"They wouldn't let me wear a hat in school. Mr. Jeffrey snatched it right off my head. And these guys won't let it go," he said, pointing at his friends.

"Yeah, I know. They look you up and down and expose your flaws."

"Like it's so funny, right?" said Brandon. "I never thought about how messed up it was before. I'd rather not go to school than have them expose my flaws."

"I'm out," said Yankee, walking up to us with his hand up. He and Brandon high-fived and Yankee raced away.

Brandon turned to me. "Are *you* okay?"

I nodded, not wanting to talk about my own problems.

"I've been trying to call you. Your phone either rang, I got a busy signal, or your father said you couldn't talk."

"Yeah, he's protective like that."

"I saw the news. He has good reason."

"Hey, I came looking for you knowing I'd miss my bus. Do you think I can catch a ride with you?"

Brandon clasped his side.

"I just have to go to my locker and get—what's wrong? Is it your stomach?"

"Nothing. I have to go." He hurried away. "Don't follow me," he said as he looked back. I was already taking a step toward him.

"But—" *I asked for a ride. His mood swings are getting on my nerves.*

TWELVE

I must've misunderstood my dad that morning, because our black Pontiac Le Mans was parked at the curb right in front of the walkway that led to the front doors of the school. The lone car in the parking lot. Had I left on the bus, he would've been looking all over for me.

"Everything okay?" he asked as I closed the car door.

"I should be asking *you* that."

"Me? Why?"

"Why aren't you at work?"

"I took some time off."

"Dad, did you get fired? Were you suspended? Because of the news? What are we doing to do? We're a one income family. How will we—"

"Riri, stop jumping to conclusions. I did not get fired. Good googly goop!" We looked at each other and laughed at him sounding like Uncle James.

I didn't hear from Brandon that night and feared he was set on staying in 1982. As far as I could tell, he was doing anything to figure out why we were back. I needed to look for clues. Dean Richard's question kept ringing in my head. I'd written that something much bigger was happening at Stoneburg. *Bigger than their form of gang violence? What did I mean? And where would I find the answers?*

My dad dropped me off at school again the next day. I think if he could have escorted me to each class, he would have. The day was pretty much the same as the previous until lunch time.

Some kids, mostly Kennedy's friends, often had a parent bring them lunch from a restaurant—McDonald's usually. The rest of us sat around jealous, smelling the French fries and wishing it could be us. Kennedy squealed loud enough for everyone in the cafeteria to turn and watch. She ran to the glass double doors. A hand reached in with a large McDonald's bag. I recognized the long high-heeled boot that stepped in after it. Mrs. Kohn.

"She's not embarrassed to show her face here?" asked Donna.

"Apparently not."

Kennedy took the bag and hugged her, while her aunt's eyes searched the cafeteria and found mine. She smiled my way. It wasn't a greeting. She wanted me to see her and acknowledge she'd be back in her position soon. "So what?" I hoped my expression said.

There were about four meals in that bag. Those who didn't know any better had to wish they were a part of her crew, as she handed burgers and fries to Calvin and Jessica, and an apple pie to Denise.

But I was more concerned that every time I saw Mrs. Kohn, the Murk was near, like they were connected. I looked all around the cafeteria, waiting for it to show itself. Its shadow was probably looming outside the exit door.

Someone tossed a gift box onto the lunch table in front of me. I was so focused on a Murk sighting that I jumped. I stared at it, but didn't turn around to see who brought it, nor did I reach for it. "Is that for you?" asked Daniel, sitting in his usual seat across from me.

"Probably."

"Are you going to open it?" asked Donna.

"Nope."

"I'll open it." He tore off the gift wrap and held it up. "A bar of soap."

A stink joke. I took it from him and tossed it in the trash. *Give it a rest already.*

As I sat down, Brandon walked in.

"Is that your friend?" asked Donna. "He cut off his long hair?"

Brandon looked around at everyone strangely and slowly turned. Something was happening. Some kind of time travel episode, I figured. The first time I came back, there were times when I went back and forth in time. Maybe that was happening to him too. Or maybe he had a memory emerge at that moment. I hopped up from my seat and hurried to him.

"Today is the day. This is the day it happened," he said. But I didn't think he was talking to anyone but himself.

"What happened?"

He suddenly noticed me. "Nothing."

"Something."

He continued to look around the room. Students were watching us. "How does your last day on earth usually start?"

"What? Are you kidding?" I motioned him over to the table to get the attention off him.

He sat and snapped out of the weird trance he'd been in. "How long were you here last time? A day? Two?" he whispered.

"Weeks."

"No..."

"Yeah, and the longer you're here..."

"What?"

"Nothing. We had that conversation already. Remember, I told you the future fades."

He sat there a moment, fidgeting with his jacket.

"Aren't you going to eat?"

"I'm on a special diet."

"Diet? You?"

"You do look thinner," someone else added.

"Eat more, not less. Aren't you in sports? You need to bulk up," Daniel said while spooning Jell-O into his mouth.

"No, I mean I can only eat certain things. Uh... allergies."

"Oh."

"Wow. That kills to be allergic to foods," said Daniel.

"And I thought it was bad that my doctor told me at my physical that I have sinuses. I don't even know what that means."

"Something stinks," said a boy next to Daniel while pinching his nose.

"Is it my breath?" I breathed into my cupped hand and sniffed. Everyone else did too.

"No. Something really stinks like poop."

We were looking around us and under the table. Brandon looked panicked and then shot out of the cafeteria holding his stomach.

"What's going on with him?" asked Donna.

"I don't know."

"He's different now," said Lisa, placing her tray on the table and taking his seat.

"He is? How?"

"Nicer. Much. I'm glad he changed. I wish the rest of them would."

"Them? As in he hung with Kennedy and those guys?"

"Yeah. I thought you knew. He was with us the night—"

"Us? What night?"

"The night we chased you."

I choked on my chocolate milk. Donna slapped my back, a little too hard, as I coughed. I had to put my hand up to stop her. I faced the girl. "Say that again."

She looked ashamed. And afraid. "I thought you knew. I mean, since you're friends with Brandon now. We were supposed to scare you. Brandon was one of us back then. But something happened, and he stopped out of nowhere."

Anger was building inside me. Here I was trying to help him and the whole time he was one of them? She had been with them too? I knew if I lifted my foot and gave her a good kick, she'd fly right off the end of the bench.

"If you were with them, then why are you an outcast now?"

"I didn't want to be like them anymore. I wanted to be like you; unafraid of people, unafraid of being yourself."

My anger subsided. "I kind of want to knock you out," I said with a grin, only half joking. But how could I stay angry at her when I had been her? Donna forgave me for how I treated her when I was one of them. I had to give this girl the same grace as well as refuge at our table.

"And you're honest. I like that."

Two days later, all the students were called to an assembly. Stoneburg had a huge auditorium. Still, it wasn't large enough for the whole high school to attend at once. Freshmen, sophomores, and some of the juniors were on the bottom floor. The rest of the juniors and seniors filled the balcony. We were taken to the theater by class and had to sit with our classmates—squeezed in together, with our teachers standing in the aisles and along the side walls. The counselors, dean, and assistant principal were on stage. To the left of them were several members of the brass section of the marching band. They blew a few notes on their instruments. Most of the students were noisy and joking around, but everyone stopped talking and looked straight ahead.

Our principal, Mr. Jeffrey, hair parted low on the side and smoothing it down as he walked, stepped up to a podium. He lectured us about how we treat one another, and asked that we go to a teacher, counselor, or dean immediately if we were being bullied or harassed in any way. "I don't care when or where it happens, find the nearest faculty member and say something. And if you see it happening to someone, say something."

My brow raised. *Really? I thought they didn't believe me.*

"Stoneburg Academy is a safe place."

Lies. Take your blinders off.

Denise, in the row in front of mine, fidgeted in her seat.

"At this time, I would like to have a moment of silence for one of our students."

What? Silence? Doesn't that mean—

I stood and looked around the auditorium for Brandon.

"Aria..." The teacher pointed at my seat. I sat while holding the back of my chair and looking over the rows of seats behind me. My heart rate increased. I felt dizzy and thought I was going to black out.

"I'm sure most of you have already heard what happened to one of our brightest students, Lisa Smith, last night."

I shot up again, but this time my "What?" was audible.

"Aria," the teacher said, and pointed again.

I sat. A girl to the right of me offered, "They say she committed suicide."

No! How? That couldn't be right.

I choked back a sob, swallowing it as if it were cod liver oil. Otherwise I would've howled and wept like a baby right there in front of everyone.

"Is that the girl who has been sitting at the lunch table with us recently?" asked Donna, leaning from behind my seat to whisper in my ear. My heart sank to the floor like an anchor from a ship. The air in the room felt thick enough to cut, as my breaths caught in my chest. I failed. No one else should have died under my watch.

But that didn't explain why they were believing there were bullies now.

The principal continued. "Lisa was a brave girl. Brave enough to document what she'd been going through."

This time I wasn't the one who gasped, but I couldn't tell who it came from.

I didn't hear much else of what was said after that. I walked back to class in a daze—numb to anything happening around me.

I barely noticed the newspapers. I don't know where they came from, but a few students in the hall and in class had a copy.

Like me, Lisa had written a letter. And like Donna, she sent it to the paper. Imagine how the Stoneburg Journal must have reacted to receive yet another letter, but from a girl who not only signed it, but committed suicide the day they received it. Her letter was printed the very next day:

I thought I was lucky. For once, I fit in. I had friends and was no longer at the bottom of the heap. Maybe that's why you let me in. You knew as much as I that I didn't belong there. And I showed it. That made it easier to manipulate and control me. Until I saw something greater: A person stronger than you who I preferred to learn from and accepted me as I was. Did you have fun laughing along with everyone else when I left the bathroom with my skirt hiked up? Did it occur to you that I didn't want everyone to see my underwear and the fact that I wore a pad? I was shaking so badly I couldn't reach and pull it down. Thank you, Aria, for helping me.

I didn't remember that.

I'm glad you had such a good laugh at my expense. That was the first sign to get out. I should have avoided you at all costs. Still, I came back to the group.

She went on to say that they were going to tell what she'd done—what they made her do—if she didn't do Calvin's homework:

'I can't get less than a C or I'm off the team,' he'd said. 'But you still have to pass exams,' I told him. 'I'll take care of that part,' he'd replied. I wondered if that meant he had means to change his grade.

I stopped reading for a moment. I knew what was coming next. When she left the group, they went after her outside of school.

She ended the letter by saying:

You should have listened to those letters that were printed in the paper. But no one wanted to think something so horrible about the city's precious private school. Had someone done something, I'd still be here. Or should I say there? Because I'm gone now, right? Why would I live? I'm better off. No one cares us. Tell my mom I'm sorry.

The teachers didn't expect us to work on lessons for that last period of the day. Some students cried. Others were stunned. Some were just quiet. I made a flower out of note paper and stuck it in Lisa's locker. I wrote on the petals: I'm sorry I failed.

THIRTEEN

My dad didn't like the way I moped around, but he understood. I tried to not look too sad because I didn't want him to worry. I saved my tears for when I was alone.

I stood at the back of the tub, waiting for the shower water to warm. It let off a cold mist as I stepped forward into the spray, no longer caring about the temperature. My hands trembled. I held a bar of Ivory soap in a washcloth, dropped them both in the tub, and broke into inconsolable tears. I grasped my arms and cried for Lisa as water sprayed over my face. But I also cried for my mom. I missed her so much.

I turned the shower off, and dried my eyes, otherwise my dad would notice when I came out. But as I dried my hair, memories of the way my mom used to help me detangle my hair surfaced. We'd banter over hair oil. I didn't want any, and she could never use enough. The 1982 me was still mourning my mom's passing and now Lisa's on top of it.

Lisa's death caused an uproar throughout the state. I was heartbroken it took someone dying to cause the public to believe my letters. Some were calling for Stoneburg Academy to be shut down.

"I'm pulling you out of that school," my dad said.

"You can't. Not yet."

"Don't tell me what I can't do."

"But I don't want to go to another school. People can change." I tried my hardest to believe the words as I said them. "Please, Dad. I need to see this through."

He looked at me oddly. "See what through?"

"I don't know. But if I fail, it never ends..." I said as I walked away.

I don't know how I knew that, but he didn't question me about it.

The morning paper often arrived at my house after I was already at school. It all depended on which paperboy was making the deliveries that day. When it was warmer, a boy would come by on his bike with a crossbody bag full of papers and chuck one at our porch. His precision was amazing. Now that it was colder, someone jumped out of the passenger side of a car and tossed it at the lawn— nowhere near the house, and often not until the afternoon. That's why I was usually one of the last to know of any new developments.

The Stoneburg Journal probably sold more newspapers than they ever did because of what they were now calling the "Red Letters." Students who never even picked up a paper before were sneaking over to the corner store to get a copy.

"Holy cow. Check this out," said a girl in the hall.

"Is it a red letter?" her friend asked. I parked myself behind them so I could listen while rummaging through my backpack. She mumbled a few lines and sucked in air.

"Bad, hunh?" asked her friend.

"Listen to this,

"'You broke that girl's arm, and I know all the other rumors about you were true too. Everyone puts up with you and makes excuses for you. I was right along with them until you turned on me after you broke out the windows of that old man's house. What did he ever do to you? Nothing. Just like I had done nothing when you bathed me in soda in the bathroom. Do you know what happens after you tease and bully and stalk someone the way you do? They spend every waking hour thinking about what you did to them and what everyone else now thinks of them and what you are going to do to them tomorrow. The teasing and taunting, the brutal attacks in the bathrooms. Nothing else matters. Who made you God over us—the one who determines how our lives should play out at school? You control, you break, you take, you lie, you steal. You're a monster. But you *will* reap what you sow.'"

"Yowzer. Who do you think it's about?" the girl asked.

You know good and well who it's about, I thought.

"I can think of only one person—or two," her friend replied.

I backed away. There it was. Kennedy's letter. But the paper had removed her name. I wondered if they weren't allowed to use a minor's name or something.

Everywhere I went, a student was shoving the newspaper at someone so they could read it.

"You know that letter is about her. Every kid at this school knows."

They were standing near the counselors' offices, huddled together.

"We need to distance ourselves from her."

"Why?"

"Someone will catch on that we've been a part of everything she's mixed up in," said Calvin. "It even mentions that old man's house. Look, if they find out it's her and start questioning people, they're going to come straight to us. You and Jessica first," he told Denise.

One of the girls pointed.

The corner of Calvin's lip curled when he turned and saw me. He was never really my friend. When I first moved to Stoneburg he was so friendly, and often sweet towards me, but forgot all about that when Kennedy was around. I bet he didn't tell anyone he asked me to be his girlfriend. I wondered what they would've thought about that, or the fact that I turned him down.

Calvin looked up and down the hall and then focused on me. "You need to stop avoiding me."

I stopped walking, faced him, and motioned with my hand for him to say whatever it was he wanted to say.

"I don't know how many letters there are, but you have to get them back. Think about someone besides yourself. Do you know what kind of trouble I'm in right now because of that girl, Lisa? I could get expelled, or worse, kicked off the team."

"I'm sure you'll figure a way to get out of it."

"My parents demanded proof she's telling the truth. That's the only reason I'm here right now."

"So let me get this straight. You don't want to get your act together and stop doing people wrong? You only want the letter back?"

He stepped closer to me and I could feel the heat emitting off him like a furnace from his anger.

"I can't go back in time and take it back."

I smirked at that. He might be the next person to have to go back and change things. "No, you can't, but do you know what you can do?"

He looked to be thinking about it. "What are you going to do, bribe me now?"

"No. I want to know what you think is the best thing to do since you can't take back what you've done."

"What? Spit it out," he exclaimed, raising his voice. He seemed to be pressing in toward me without even moving.

"Something that obviously never crossed your mind. Apologize. And stop."

I walked away. The sound of him hitting a door echoed throughout the corridor. A counselor approached, asking what was going on.

Sorry, Calvin. Those letters are out of my hands. But unlike Kennedy's letter, no one would know his letter was about him.

Now they were seeing what it was like to be us, fearing for what might happen the next day at school.

Conveniently, Kennedy was nowhere to be found.

Brandon never came back to the lunchroom that day he ran out, and I'd looked for him ever since.

After school, out of nowhere, I heard his voice.

"Aria," he yelled, as if nothing had ever happened.

"Don't talk to me!"

"Why?"

"First of all, where the heck have you been? Are you avoiding me? Are you trying to stay here forever?"

"Forever? No one wants to be at school forever. What's wrong with you?" asked Tracey, passing by.

I lowered my voice. "Second, you're a liar."

"What are you talking about?"

"You told me you barely remembered Calvin. I believed you. You lied to me."

"No, I didn't. I only told you what I remembered." At least that part I knew was true because the first time I came back to 1982, I didn't remember everything either.

"Why were you friends with them?"

"Shh…"

"Don't shush me!" Brandon grabbed my hand, and I yanked it away from him.

"Okay, hold on. What can I say?"

"The truth."

"I don't make friends easily. If you walked into a classroom, the gym, or cafeteria and saw me, you wouldn't say, 'Him. That kid right there. I want to know him.' You wouldn't choose me over everyone else."

"So?"

"They accepted me. I became cool because of them."

"Cool how?"

"Fonzie cool."

Did he just reference the Happy Days show? I wanted to laugh but I couldn't I was angry and had to keep a straight face.

"You chased me…" I lowered my voice, "that night."

"I don't remember that—I mean I didn't remember at first. Not until I was at your house. Remember I said, 'I know why it's coming for me now…' I didn't know what to say or do, so I left."

My voice shook. All the emotions of that night poured in, filling me as if it had just happened. "I never disliked anyone. I never compared myself to anyone. Like kids do, I just lived. Why would that make someone dislike me so much?"

"Aria, I'm sorry. I don't know what to say about the boy I was then, but I apologize. I was stupid."

"Yeah, you're stupid all right," said Kennedy in passing while flipping her hair over her shoulder.

Brandon turned to her. "You know what? I'm so sick of you—you and your gang." He lowered his voice, but I heard him loud and clear. "Maybe someone should tell the newspaper about your little clubhouse. You know, the one where you hide your stolen items?"

What?

"Be careful," she said, speaking louder than he had.

"It doesn't matter how pretty you are on the outside. If you are a kind, caring person, it makes you beautiful. If you're mean and evil, it makes you ugly. Which do you think you are?"

"Ha!" I exclaimed. It was about time someone stood up to her—other than me.

Everyone in the hall stopped walking, talking, and no one laughed.

Brandon was the type of boy who didn't fight girls. I could see that. But for a second, I wished he wasn't such a gentleman and would sock her in the eye.

Kennedy stepped toward me, and Donna dashed in between us. "If we're dancing, then I'm cutting in." *Where did she get that line?* Donna was never embarrassed to say corny stuff like that.

"Stay out of this, Donna, with your ugly self. No one is even talking to you."

"Don't talk to her like that."

"I may be the most unattractive girl in the school. But at least I'm not the most hated," Donna replied.

"Break it up! What's going on down there?" asked Dean Richards. "Aria?"

"Nothing."

"My office. All of you," he called from up the hall.

"What did I just witness out there? I want the truth. What's going on with all of you?"

"Nothing," said Brandon.

We all sat around a small conference room table. The room was stuffy, and my throat was dry. I wanted to ask if I could go to the water fountain just outside the door to get some air but thought against it. Kennedy would either lie on me while I was gone or stick her foot out and trip me on my way out.

"I want answers. If you tell me nothing again, I will have no choice but to expel you. All of you."

Nice try, Dean Richards, but as you can see, our poker faces are solid.

"Donna, I'm not used to seeing you involved in an altercation. What happened and don't tell me 'nothing.'"

"She started it," she replied, staring hard at Kennedy.

"I did not."

"You always start it," I chimed in.

"Brandon?"

"Talk to Kennedy."

"Alright then, Kennedy?"

She began to speak and then broke into tears. The nerve. "I was just..." She seemed to overcome to continue. I really didn't think she had anything else to say. That's why she let the fake tears take over.

"Hmm..." Dean Richards handed her tissues from the bookshelf behind him. "I'm sorry you're so upset, Kennedy. But considering everything that's been happening around here, no one is leaving until I get answers."

He wasn't lying. He kept us in that room until well after school hours. Until I told him, "It was an argument. She called him stupid," I said while pointing at Kennedy, "and Donna, ugly. That's all that happened before you spotted us. We were defending ourselves with words only."

Brandon agreed.

"Interesting. That doesn't explain the breakdown you had a moment ago, Kennedy."

She looked startled.

"I think I'm going to call each of your parents today."

"Okay," I replied, nonchalant.

"No," said Kennedy.

"No?" Dean Richards repeated.

"I mean, I apologize." She turned to each of us. "I'm sorry about what I said. I didn't mean it—any of it."

Dean Richards looked pleased. "I appreciate you doing that. You may leave."

It's about time, I thought as our chairs screeched across the floor as we pushed them back and stood.

"Not you, Kennedy. Have a seat."

I followed Brandon and Donna out of the office in silence. All the students were gone for the day, leaving the school feeling abandoned.

"What was that about?" asked Donna.

"You mean Kennedy? I don't know, but she sure didn't want her parents knowing about what happened. Can I get a ride home? Will your mom mind?"

"Of course not."

"Will she mind one more?" asked Brandon.

"I'm sure she won't," said Donna.

I nudged him. "As long as you don't talk to me. I haven't forgotten about what you did..."

FOURTEEN

Some days since my return, '80s music got on my nerves. Especially when there was a fast thump, thump, thump, like the bass player only knew one or two notes. There were so many songs like that.

I turned the knob on my radio, looking for a better song, and settled on Zapp's "More Bounce to the Ounce."

"I'm leaving, Riri," yelled my dad.

"Okay!"

"Aria!"

"I know, I'm turning it down."

As soon as I lowered the volume, I found the phone ringing. I guess it *was* too loud.

"Hello?"

"Aria, it's me. Don't hang up!" Brandon exclaimed. He was panting. "You were right. I need your help. Get me out of here—back to 1990, I mean. That thing is after me. Tell me what to do."

That thing? The Murk? "Slow down. Where are you?"

"I'm at a payphone near the meat store not far from your neighborhood."

"Acres?"

"Yeah."

"Stay right there. I'm coming."

I don't know what I thought I could do to help. But if I was like the owl, and it saved *me* once, maybe I could do the same for him. Yes, I was angry with Brandon, but I refused to fail him like I had Lisa.

I grabbed each end of a bandana, made fast circles, and wrapped the tightly wound band across my forehead and tied it in back. Then I snatched it off my head. *What are you doing? This is no time to try to be cute.* I pulled on a skullcap beanie and my coat and searched for a flashlight. Actually, I threw a bunch of stuff in my pockets, not knowing what I might need, including a shell from my dad's shotgun. I guess I was going to throw it at the Murk.

Due to the approaching winter storm, my father got called into work. Winter was a busy time for electric companies due to power outages. My dad told me the demand for power went up exponentially because everyone turned up the heat to stay warm. When that happened, the wires get heated and the amount of power going through them causes them to droop like a loose rubber band. Those wires aren't supposed to touch and can trigger an explosion.

"Even if they don't touch each other, if they so much as droop onto trees, POW!" He knew I would jump, and he laughed his head off. By the time I graduated high school, I'd probably know more about the power company and how electricity worked than any other teen.

My father did not allow me to do out when he worked nights. He'd call and check on me throughout the night to make sure I was okay, so I took the phone off the hook. Donna and I always tied up the line, so getting a busy signal was normal.

I ran down the street, through a field, and across a busy intersection.

"Brandon!" I ran past storefront windows calling his name. The lights were on, but no one was inside.

"I'm here," He said as he stepped into view from the side of the building.

"What happened?"

His teeth chattered. He'd been out there a long time. At least that's why I thought they chattered. "My dad was riding me about-about…" He seemed to shake off the thought and continued. "I needed to get out of there. He told me I'd better not leave the house, but I was like, 'I'm a grown man.' I forgot I'm only fourteen. I left anyway."

"You live around here?"

"No, off Pierce. I started walking and before I knew it, I was all the way over here. Then—"

We looked behind us. The wind howled and there was what sounded like millions of wings flapping, although there was nothing there.

"It's coming."

"There!" I pointed. "Go there." We ran and ducked along the back side of the outdoor bleachers of an elementary school's baseball field and waited.

"We're still out in the open." Brandon blew inside his gloves. "What are you doing?"

"Praying."

"I hope it helps."

We squatted. "My house isn't far. I think we should make a run for it."

"No," he stuttered. "This thing is powerful. I lied before. I've heard it in my head, just like you said. This menacing voice filling me with thoughts that I don't even want to repeat. And I've been getting really depressed. My father says I'm withdrawn. Whatever that means."

"That's it. That's what it does. That's how it will get you to—"

"To what?"

"Exactly what Lisa did. What I almost did." I stood. "Come on. Let's go."

"I can't move."

"You were just moving."

"I can't now."

"Okay. Take deep breaths. We'll wait." I might not have shown it as much as Brandon did, but I was just as afraid.

I couldn't think of any way to calm him down other than getting him to talk more. I knelt beside him. "In the future, your ear is pierced. Do you remember that?"

He thought for a moment. "Yes. My left ear."

"I noticed a lot of guys with their ear pierced. I guess that's what's in fashion in 1990?"

"That's not why I did it."

"Oh, why did you do it then?"

"It is an ancient Chinese belief that the wearing of an earring in the left ear symbolizes a person's life has been endangered, and to prevent a recurrence, an earring is worn to ward off bad luck."

"Endangered? That's why you have it? How—"

"Before you ask, I have no idea. I can't remember."

"Could it be—" I pointed at his stomach.

"How do you know about that?"

"You. You're always clutching it. But I don't know why."

"Some things are not easy to deal with."

"What is it?"

He sighed. "Crohn's disease. I have a temporary colostomy bag."

"I don't know what that means."

"It means my intestines are temporarily rerouted to my stomach. And there is a bag that collects—"

He could see from my wide eyes I knew what he was talking about. "I've done everything I can to keep it a secret until I have surgery."

"So that smell at the lunch table?"

"The bag broke. I keep a second uniform and everything I need in the nurse's station."

I grabbed his arm. "Oh my gosh." And I thought *I* had problems. I didn't know what else to say. I felt so bad for him. "When is your surgery?"

"I don't know. That's what my argument with my dad was about, because I want it immediately. And if everyone at school finds out—"

"It's going to be okay, Brandon. It won't always be this way. Kids don't understand."

"But you do."

"Yeah…"

"You're different."

"Why, because I'm practically bald?"

"No. Because you have a heart. And you're the only girl in woodwork class."

"How did you know that? You're not in my class."

"This kid, Lonnie."

"Well, I *am* different, and proud of it."

The longer I talked to him, the more he calmed. "No matter how we are connected, something has to be undone. That's the reason you are here. I'm afraid I haven't been the best guide. I don't think I've helped you at all. I'm not even certain what I'm supposed to do."

"You have. You've been explaining things. There's not a lot you can do if this journey is about *my* life. But it helps that I'm not alone. Are you still mad at me?"

"Under the circumstances, you can have a pass." I grinned nervously. "At school you said this is the day it happens. You were talking to yourself. What was supposed to happen?"

I heard a clunk and then his scream, as his head fell back against the risers.

"Brandon!" I shook him and shined my flashlight in his face. His screech subsided. He knocked me back and ran off into the field.

"Where are you going!" I pumped my arms and ran as fast as I could, trying to catch him. His pace slowed, and he stopped, no longer worried about the Murk getting to him.

"The day it happened," he said as he turned in a circle, chanting it over and over as he looked around. He stopped and pointed a gloved finger at me. "You stopped it. You saved me."

I approached him with my arms outstretched. "What was that? Why were you screaming?"

"I just relived what happened to me that day—I mean, the first time. It didn't happen, because you changed things."

"How? What was it?" I couldn't imagine what would've made him scream out in agony like that.

"Calvin would've exposed me. My stomach. In front of everyone."

"Are you certain?" Even that seemed more than I'd expect from him.

"Yes. After school. We-we got into a fight."

"Oh, no."

"You stopped it." His eyes pleaded with me. "Can we go back now?"

"I don't know. Take my hand, like we did on the dorm roof."

We took our gloves off. I extended my hand, and he grasped it, firm. We stood there for a moment, waiting.

"Do you feel anything?" he asked.

"I—"

Just past Brandon, a shadowy smoky glob rose from the ground, blotting out the neighborhood behind it. Brandon had been watching our hands. He looked up at me and slowly turned. I let go of his hand and stepped in front of him. "Run!" I yelled.

Brandon didn't move.

"He made his choice," a voice growled.

"He deserves a second chance!" I said, sounding almost brave.

"It's too late!"

"No, it's not!"

The area around me began to shift. "No!" I screamed. "Not now!"

I reached for Brandon as his image blurred into everything else.

"Quiet yourself," a gentle voice said as I floated. "You can't receive the truth, for the noise. It's *his* journey."

"I know, but I can't just leave him. He needs my help. I have to go back!"

It didn't matter what I said or how I pleaded. Within seconds, I was back in 1990 on the college campus, looking over the roof at the neighboring dorms. Leaves blew over the courtyard as students, oblivious to the mysteries of the world, passed by.

I looked at the spot where Brandon had stood. "There's still time. There has to be."

I ran to the door, down the stairs, and to the end of the hall on the top floor to a payphone. I hardly ever carried change, but I searched my pockets. I pulled out a few coins and dug out two dimes and a nickel from below the pennies and placed them in the slot. The phone rang several times. Just as I was about to hang up, I heard her voice.

"Hello?" She sounded out of breath, as if she'd been running to catch it.

"Donna, is that you?"

"Of course it is."

"What day and time is it—oh, and the year? When did you see me last?"

"Whoa, are you saying you're back again? I just saw you today, and you said you just came back."

"So I always come back right where I left off then?"

"I don't know."

"Sorry, I was thinking aloud. I wasn't really asking you."

"You need one of those watches that has a date and time on it."

"Good idea. You will not believe what just happened."

"Where are you?"

"The Commons."

"Stay there. I'm on my way."

"Gotcha!"

I jumped. "Oh my gosh, you startled me." I motioned Donna to a wrought-iron bench and studied her face as if I hadn't seen her since ninth grade. "I can't get over how beautiful you are."

She blushed. "Stop it before you give me a big head."

"It's already big," I joked. "Close your eyes."

"Why? Do you have a surprise for me?"

"I want you to think back to 1982. Tell me what you remember about ninth grade."

"I have to close my eyes for that?"

"It will help you focus."

She turned her floppy hat up in front and faced me with her eyes closed. "Okay, Stoneburg sucked."

"We know that. For real, think."

"We were friends. The letters. Oh my gosh!"

"What?"

She opened her eyes and looked over her round sunglasses. "Someone died."

I nodded at her. "I have to get back there."

FIFTEEN

"Where are we going?" asked Donna.

"I'm supposed to meet someone at the Library at eight. His name is Lonnie. I think he can help. He attended Stoneburg Academy as well."

We searched the first floor of the library and then went up to the second floor.

"Is that him with the curly hi-top?" asked Donna.

"Yeah."

Lonnie sat at a table near the windows. He pretended to study, looking up from his book every few minutes for me.

"Go." She pushed me toward him.

"Hey, Lonnie."

"Aria, hello. I-I'm glad you came. Weren't you coming to study—alone?"

"I was, but something has come up. Something important. I was hoping you could help me with it."

"I can try. Hello, friend who came along in case I'm a lunatic."

"No, it's not like that."

"That's something I would do, though," said Donna.

"Not helping," I whispered. "Lonnie, I need a big favor."

"I'm listening."

"Were you leaving your dorm when we ran into each other earlier?"

"Why?"

"I need to get into someone's room."

"Why would I help you get into another guy's room?"

I glanced at Donna. "Did I say he was a guy?"

Donna shrugged.

"Because uh, because..."

"He stole something from her, but it was really mine, and my mother is going to flip out when she learns I've lost it," Donna replied.

"Then call—"

"No, no, we don't want him to get in trouble. That could ruin his future. I just want my bracelet back."

"So what will you do if I say no?"

"Umm... We'll have to break in," I said matter-of-factly.

"Yeah," Donna replied.

He studied us for a moment. "Okay, sounds like trouble, but I'll do it. I didn't feel like studying, anyway."

If he decided to help us so I'd like him, it was working.

Lonnie grabbed his books from the table and followed us out of the library and down the walk. We had quite a trek to the back of campus where the dorms were.

"Hey, what happened to your accent?" he asked.

"Excuse me?"

"You used to have a New York accent. Drove us guys crazy. Everyone wanted to talk to you."

"That's a shock."

"Did you expect them to tell you that? Guys don't do that. That boogie-down Bronx thing was so different."

I laughed. "I'm not from the 'boogie-down Bronx.' I'm from Brooklyn. Anyway, I'm a Michigander now. But I will always be a New Yorker at heart. Did we have classes together?"

"Not until sophomore year, and I'm insulted you don't remember," he joked.

"Then how did you know me from freshman year?"

"I saw you around."

"But you knew about my accent."

"Shouldn't we focus on what we're about to do here?" he asked, embarrassed.

I pointed at Donna. "What about her? Do you remember her? Did you see her around too?"

"You went to Stoneburg?"

"Yep."

"I guess that answers that question."

He led us inside Munson Hall. "Who are we looking for?"

"Brandon. Brandon…" *Why don't I ever know his last name?*

"I know you don't mean Brandon from Stoney?"

"Stoney? Who called Stoneburg Academy that?"

"Everybody."

I looked at Donna. "Seniors," she replied.

"Oh, but yes. Brandon from Stoney. He's in my speech class. Did you know him at Stoney?"

"Let's take the elevator. Yeah, I knew him. We weren't buddy-buddy. But we knew each other." The elevator stopped on the fourth floor. Lonnie pointed and held the door as we exited first. "That's his room." He looked up the hall and pulled a credit card from his wallet. "When I get it open, just hurry and get your bracelet and let's get out of here. You guys are going to owe me for this."

"Hey, wait," I said, grabbing his arm.

"Having second thoughts?"

"Umm…"

"How about telling me why we're really here?"

We weren't very good liars. And that wasn't a bad thing. "Brandon is in trouble and we're trying to help him."

"Then we should go to campus security."

"It's too personal for that. Lonnie, what do you remember about Brandon? Is he the same person he was in high school?"

L. B. ANNE

He backed up and leaned against the wall, I guess contemplating everything I'd said. "Okay. He was cool. Popular. Then he got dark."

"What do you mean?"

"You know, like some of the punk kids? It seemed like he hated everyone. Something happened to him… Wait a minute." He jogged down the hall and banged on a door. "Terrence! Open up, man. It's the PoPo!"

Terrence opened the door, laughing. "You play too much!"

He pointed across the hall. "Brandon. You remember what happened to him at Stoney?"

Did everyone from Stoneburg choose this University?

"Wasn't he in a fire or something? No, he jumped off a building, right?"

"What?" I pulled Donna. "We've gotta go."

Lonnie held up his credit card and pointed toward Brandon's room. "But what about?"

"Don't worry about it."

"I hope you find—"

I didn't hear the rest. I was already running into the stairwell and down the steps.

"What are you thinking? What are you going to do?" asked Donna from behind me.

"I need to call my dad. I'll see you later."

"But—"

134

I dashed out the door. Maybe my dad remembered something from the news from back then. I called, but his answering machine picked up.

A couple of hours later, Donna ran into our dorm room. "Hey, you're here. Good. Take a look at this." She pushed papers toward me.

I read the top page and flipped over to the next. "Where did you get this?" I jumped from my desk chair and hugged her.

"The newspaper archives."

My hand covered my mouth as I looked up at her and back at the paper.

"I know," she responded as if I'd asked a question.

"Stoneburg was known as the suicide school?"

She nodded. "The suicide school."

"When did it start?"

"Turn the page."

My hand shook as my finger followed a line of text. I don't know why I was so anxious. My hands dropped to my lap. "They listed the names. Did you read them?"

"Yours isn't there."

"No, but Brandon's is. How is it there when he's alive now?"

"Alive, but nowhere to be found?"

My eyes widened.

Donna turned the page. "Keep reading."

"What? This can't be right.

"Kennedy is on the list?"

SIXTEEN

I spent every moment trying to figure out how to get back to 1982. Mostly for Brandon. But now there was Kennedy. I didn't like her. I was still holding on to the feelings associated with the memories of Stoneburg. I hadn't been back that long, so it was all so fresh. A part of me didn't care what was going to happen to her. But of all people, *her*? The most popular person in the school? No, it was a different Kennedy. It had to be.

Donna watched me at my desk from her bunk. "I can see you're still trying to figure this out. I feel like there's a reason bigger than Brandon, why you went back. We didn't know it at the time, but that's why those letters you wrote—"

"That *you* sent in to the newspaper—"

"Yes, but we're past that. That's why they triggered so much."

"Possibly," I said as I climbed in bed. "Goodnight."

I closed my eyes, but I couldn't sleep. I twisted and turned all night.

My alarm clock blinked 3:45 am. *I have to go back.* I hopped up, grabbed my backpack, and stuffed clothes in. Donna awoke, rubbing her eyes. "What are you doing? Where are you going?"

"Stoneburg."

"Really? Right now?"

"Yes."

She sat up. "Let me get dressed. I'm coming with you."

I pulled my ponytail through the back of my baseball cap. "No. I need you to stay here."

"Are you sure?"

"Yes.

"I'll keep doing research."

"Let me know about anything you find out."

"I will." She hugged me. "Aria, remember that thing— the dark force you told me about? What if it's controlling what happens? All the evil that's there—affecting the kids."

"You could be right about that."

I pulled the hood of my sweater over my head and hopped from one foot to the other, trying to say warm. "Donna, it's me."

"Where are you?"

"I stopped at a rest area. I'm checking in to see if you found out anything else."

"As a matter of fact, I have. Thank goodness the library opened early because we're going into finals week. I was waiting there when the door opened and—"

"Donna…"

"Okay, let me get to the point. The Kohns. Kennedy's family? They have been a part of Stoneburg forever. Like high society. Mrs. Kohn's father was the principal in the late sixties. That's Kennedy's grandfather. But there has always been something dark associated with them. You should see the microfilm. Not a happy bunch."

"But was it considered the suicide school for all those years?"

"Not that I can tell. It seems like it began around 1980."

"Was Mrs. Kohn working there then?"

"Yep. And I know that because I was there in seventh grade."

So it's connected to Mrs. Kohn. "Thanks, Donna. I'm going to get back on the road."

"Be careful."

The drive through downtown Stoneburg brought back memories, and not all were bad. The bridge over the river reminded me of the river cruise I'd taken with my dad. I missed that part of my youth. We called each other a lot, Him telling me to make sure I always had gas in my car or fussing about how long it had been since I had an oil change. But we hardly saw each other.

My gas gauge was on E. Well, it had been for a while, but I knew the tank wasn't empty. I could probably make it twenty more miles but chose not to chance it. If I ran out of gas, I'd never hear the end of it from my dad.

I pulled over at a station and hopped out of my Volkswagen Jetta. She was my baby. I'd scrimped and saved to get her.

"Aria, is that you?" asked a muscular guy at the next gas pump.

"Do I know you?"

"It's me, Calvin."

Calvin? From Stoneburg Academy? What's he doing here? Didn't he go off to college out of state somewhere?

"Wow, you look good," he said. "I haven't seen you in years. How are you?"

"I'm fine."

"Good. That's good... You know, I always wanted to apologize to you."

"Why didn't you?"

"As you know, I was a bit out-of-control back then. I'm just—I'm so sorry."

"I appreciate that. It would have meant so much more back then but thank you." *Shut up, Aria,* I thought, shaking my head at myself. "Have you seen anyone else from the Academy?"

"Nah, after the fire, we all kind of went our separate ways."

"Fire?" *Another mention of a fire.*

"How could you forget the fire? What was his name? Brandon. Yeah, he went berserk."

"What?"

"Listen, I have to go to work, but maybe we can catch up later."

"Let's do that," I replied. "We're still at the same house." Now that he was so apologetic, maybe he had information that could help me.

"Cool, see you later."

While watching him pull away, a memory surfaced, instantly transporting me back to a day when I was walking down Clio Road to catch the city bus. I remembered I was bundled up, but the cold air seemed to go right through me. *Ten, eleven, twelve*, I counted. Something I often did as I walked while making sure I didn't step on a crack. "Aria," Calvin called. He pulled up beside me in a car with three other boys. An older boy was driving.

"Hey, Calvin," I'd said.

"Get in, we'll give you a ride to school."

"No, that's okay."

"I know you're freezing. We're all going to the same place." He looked back at the boys, grinning. The car pulled beside a fire hydrant. Calvin hopped out of the front passenger seat, leaving the door open, and sat in the back.

"Get in," said the driver. "Hurry up, girl. Don't make us come out after you."

"He's just joking, New York," said Calvin. "Let's go."

I slowly walked over.

"You're going to make us all late!"

I got in the car, a white Regal. I hated Regals after that day. We drove off with me sitting right against the door.

"Relax."

I don't know why I couldn't. Maybe it was because I was in a car with a bunch of strange boys, or because I noticed we were going the wrong way. "This isn't the way to school."

"It's okay. I need to stop at my Uncle's house real quick." the driver said.

"No. I need to get to school. Pull over so I can get out."

"I'm not stopping this car. You can leave when we get there if you like."

There was no way I was going to that house with them. I looked for an opportunity to flee, but they watched me whenever we came to a red light. So after the next red light, I opened the door while the car was still moving.

"Hey, close the door."

The car slowed. I acted like I was reaching for the handle to close it and jumped out. I ran as fast as my legs would take me.

"Are you okay?" asked the gas station attendant, walking toward me. I was still holding onto the pump.

"Yes, I've got a lot on my mind."

"Looks that way," he said.

How had I forgotten that happened?

Instead of going to my dad's house like I'd planned, I drove straight to Stoneburg Academy. More memories flooded my brain as I ran up the walk. Memories about everything except Brandon.

The main doors were unlocked, and first period had started, so the corridors were empty. The place hadn't changed a bit. Same dark paint on the brick of the lower walls. Pale blue on the upper wall.

Come on, Aria, remember. What happened here? What happened to Brandon?

I stood there, looking in the display case at state championship trophies and team photos from the last few years. The building still had that school smell. What was that anyway, disinfectant? I heard something behind me and turned, expecting to see a teacher or office staff.

It can't be.

It was right there. The snowy owl. I was relieved and terrified at the same time. Time seemed to slow as it flew down the hall toward me, its wingspan filling the width of the corridor. Even from a distance, its piercing yellow eyes were pulling me in. I couldn't move or turn away. It was going to slam into me. I wanted to duck, but I couldn't move. Just as we collided, it passed right through me and I was immediately floating back through time.

That gentle voice spoke: "They are allowing themselves to become stuck in oppression and condemnation. It has to stop, or your generation will become unfruitful."

"But how can I help Brandon—the whole school? Why did I have to come back?"

"You're putting yourselves in the same positions. It should not be. You must help them... Overcome." That last word echoed as I was transported back to 1980.

SEVENTEEN

Howard Johnson's "So Fine" blared throughout the house. It was my favorite song. I sat on my bed staring at the radio. *Okay, you've got my attention, owl. I'm back, but when? Am I too late?*

I turned the knob, lowering the volume. My dad would soon scream for me to turn it down anyway and complain about me having no hearing by the time I'm fifty. Instead he yelled, "Aria, you have company!"

Brandon. "You must help them overcome," echoed in my head.

Got it. Overcome.

I hurried to the living room. "Donna, hey." I tried to act cool. I didn't want to seem surprised to see her if we'd already had the conversation that she was coming over. "Let's go down to—" I abruptly stopped talking.

"What are you doing here, Denise?"

Toya walked in behind her. "You two need to talk," she said.

"I don't think so."

Denise held her letter up. "I deserved this. I didn't realize how bad it was until I received it."

"Yes, you did." I sat on the arm of our sofa and crossed my arms in front of me.

"Can we sit?"

"Go ahead. It's a free country."

Donna and Toya sat beside me. Denise sat in the chair across from us. "Who else did you send one to?"

Wait, is this before all the letters came out?

"I mean, besides those in the paper?"

Which has been printed so far? "Did Kennedy send you here to question me? Do you enjoy being her puppet?"

"It's not like that. At least not anymore."

"Since when?"

"She's so mad. And says you're trying to destroy everything and everybody. And she doesn't like that you're chummy with her ex-friend."

"Lisa?"

"Yeah."

Did I go back to before...? My heart pounded hard and fast. "When was the last time you saw her?"

"Kennedy?

"No, Lisa."

"Today. Why?"

I exhaled and rubbed my hands over my legs. "I just wondered. Donna, why are you with them?"

"Denise came to me."

"I didn't think you would talk to me without her and Toya." Denise's voice was trembling.

"She's not hanging with them anymore," said Toya.

"Since when?"

"Since someone hurt my little brother."

"Today, at school?"

Toya nodded. "He saw something he shouldn't have."

"Is he okay?"

"He will be."

"I'm sorry. He didn't deserve that." I almost reached out and touched her as she stared at the hardwood floor. "You're upset right now, but you know as well as I do, you're going to go right back to them. You can't live in both worlds, you know. You're either with us or them. That's all there is."

"If I'm with you, will my letter be in the paper?"

I stood. "I knew it. You can leave now."

Denise leapt from the chair. "I just wanted to know. Here. Look. I don't care who reads it." She scrambled to unfold the letter and handed it to Toya to read. To my surprise, she began to cry and crumbled into Donna on the sofa. "I'm so tired of all of this."

Donna put an arm around her and looked up at me with an expression that asked, *what am I supposed to do?*

The next day, I walked out of study hall and saw the usual crew hanging out together, but there was no Denise. Maybe she was telling the truth.

"Look at them. Watch this," said Kennedy. "I'm bored. I'm going to make something happen." Then she saw me.

"Go for it. What are you going to do?" Jessica asked with a laugh. "Do it."

Kennedy didn't move. Jessica turned. "Oh, it's her. Keep it moving."

And I did. Confrontations would only waste what time I had to set things straight. Now I was on a mission to conclude this journey as fast as possible with no casualties.

Jessica made squawking sounds as I passed—I guess calling me a bird again. She just would not let up. But that afternoon, her attitude went from bad to malicious. Another "Red Letter" was printed in the paper:

You soaked my sweater with perfume and started the stink rumor. I guess I got off easy because I know you set another student's clothes on fire outside while she was in gym class. You look for reasons to start fights with people. But you don't work alone. You all surrounded me so you could plant the punch to my stomach. But that wasn't the worst part. The worst part was you making fun of a person with a disease. "Look at her mother. Freaks." Remember that? Do you remember what you said to me? "That's why your mom is dead. You should go and be with her." Who would say that to someone who just returned to school after her mother's passing? It was thoughtless and cruel, but that's who you are.

I heard a scream from the locker room. "Shh..." someone said. "No one knows it's about you."

"I'm gonna get her," she growled. "She's not going to get away with this. Why are we letting her live?"

Letting her live?

"What?" Lisa was passing by and stopped. "Why did you say that?"

Oh no.

"What did you hear?"

Lisa didn't respond.

"You better keep your mouth shut or—"

"Or what?" I asked as I followed them into the gym. We had to go through the gym to get out to the main hall. "She doesn't have to say anything. I heard you myself. Let me live?"

"I didn't say that."

"You better watch your back," Jessica told Lisa.

"You just threatened her, in front of people."

"No, I didn't."

"You did. I heard you."

"I heard you too," said Denise.

Jessica's mouth dropped.

"I heard you," Daniel and four other kids repeated.

She walked away. "I'll see you later, Lisa."

"No, you won't," I replied and held Lisa back so everyone else could pass.

"That was so awesome. We all stuck together. That's the way it should always be," said a girl, Tracey. I did kind of wish Donna had been there to witness it.

"Tracey, calm down." She was jumping with excitement. "Guys, let me talk to Lisa a minute."

Her eyes were watering. "That was nice of you, but they're going to get me."

"No, they aren't. You can't live in fear like this. Give me your number and here's mine. Call me at any time. Where is your last class?"

"In the two-hundred hall with Mrs. Stamps."

"I will meet you there. Don't leave the room until I arrive."

She nodded.

Our little bodyguard group walked her to her class. We didn't know, but we were starting something that students would implement for years to come at Stoneburg.

"Donna!" Daniel exclaimed, calling her over. "You missed it."

"What happened?"

"We stood together against Jessica."

"It was epic," said Tracey.

She looked at me for confirmation of what they were saying. "It's true."

"Tell me everything later, I've gotta go. I'll see you later," said Donna.

"Where—"

"I have to meet someone really quick about a thing."

"What does that mean?" I asked, but she hurried off. I watched everyone go their separate ways and even waved back at Denise. Maybe she *was* really done with Kennedy.

Before I could take two steps, that feeling of doom came over me, slowly swallowing me, like quicksand. I sighed. Lisa wasn't as strong as me. I had to prevent her from choosing to do something to end her life.

You know what you have to do, I told myself. There was only one way to save Lisa.

I ran down the hall and burst into Dean Richards' office.

"I need to talk to you."

He waved away Mrs. Wallace.

I handed him a piece of paper and cleared my throat. "I know you're wondering who the letters in the paper were written to. Those are the students."

EIGHTEEN

"Thank you, Aria." That's all that Dean Richards said. I wanted him to fill me in. What were the next steps? What would he do? I wanted all the details, but he took the note and sent me on my way. And there was no surprise in his expression as I rattled off the list.

So what was I to do? I went to class, turned in my current events assignment, and planned how Lisa would get home safely. My teacher, Mr. Riley, snapped his fingers in my face. "I need you paying attention, Aria." I sat up and focused on the blackboard and even raised my hand to answer a question. Then I figured I'd given him enough attention and settled back into my thoughts.

I was the first one out of my seat when class was over. Daniel and I approached Lisa at the same time. "You got her?" he asked.

"Yes, thanks."

"No sweat."

I walked Lisa out to the parking lot. Donna's mom pulled up in front of the school. Donna ran over and opened the station wagon passenger door. "Mom, can we give her a ride home?"

"But I just live—" Lisa pointed.

"Believe me, you don't want to walk," I told her.

I could see Donna's mom nodding. "She said yes. Go."

"Thanks, Aria," said Lisa.

Kennedy's goons were already outside watching, waiting to chase after her like they did me the day I hid in the corner store.

Not today, girls, and hopefully, never again.

I stared at myself in the mirror that evening. *"Why are we letting her live,"* Jessica had said. *Did that mean they hadn't let someone else live before? The suicide school.* I could see it now. That's what they pushed kids to. Whoever Mrs. Kohn instructed had to go, they broke to the point of suicide. Was that what was happening? I had to be sure.

"What are you doing?" My dad asked, trying not to laugh.

While I was thinking, I'd taken two short strands of hair and twisted them together. I turned to him with the tiny twist sticking straight up. "It's almost long enough to put a barrette on it."

He laughed, walked into the bathroom, and tugged at my little lock.

"Dad, no!" I exclaimed, seeing his skin.

"What?"

My father walked around in so many layers, I'd forget what his body looked like. He wore thermals, flannels, t-shirts, and three pairs of socks. But this day he was in a t-shirt and no socks. He'd made a quick trek in a slow-motion jog to the kitchen to get his coffee before he layered up.

"Look at you. You're so ashy. You need lotion."

"Is it that bad?" He laughed.

"Yes. Your elbows are white and I'm not even going to bring up that area between your toes."

He looked down. "I'll get the Vaseline."

"You can't oil up and then put clothes over it. That's so gross."

"Well, how do you want me, oily or ashy?"

"Put it on before bed."

"Then I'm oily in the bed. That's what's gross."

I threw my hands up. "I give up. Where are you going?"

"I'm going to put on this robe of mine you keep confiscating," he said as he reached behind the door, "and put on some socks, and then it's *Little House on the Prairie* time. Are you coming?"

"Let's do something else."

"You only want to listen to music or watch MTV."

"That's what teens do. It wouldn't hurt you to move a little. It keeps you young."

"All right."

"All right?"

"Sure. I'll dance with you and you watch the show with me."

I was in shock, but I was excited to take him on. "One second. Let me make one call."

"I know your calls. You've got three minutes."

I dialed fast. She picked up on the first ring.

"Hello?"

"Who is he?" I asked.

"Dang it, Aria. Hello to you too. How do you always know stuff?"

"I have to meet someone really quick about a thing?"

"Was that code for there's a guy? His name is Billy. William, but Billy. It was supposed to be a secret."

"From me?"

"No. Yes. I mean, from everyone for now."

The phone beeped as someone punched buttons. "Dad, you know I'm on the phone."

"Oh, I need to use it."

"You don't have to say that into the phone. You could just hang up. See, this is why I need my own private line." I knew he was really trying to tell me my three minutes were up.

"All right then. Hello Donna," he said and hung up.

"Have you guys been to Taco Bell together?" I asked.

"How did you know that?"

"I have eyes everywhere. I've gotta go. Carry on with Billy," I told her, and hung up. I was happy for her. Billy might help her to hold her head up high and not always worry about what people thought of her mouth.

"Okay, father. I'm ready."

"Father?" he repeated with a laugh. "My show first. MTV after."

"Deal."

It was a fun night, and funny how excruciating it was for my dad to watch some of the music videos. I'd created a great memory for us. A little joy was necessary due to the fallout I knew was coming from giving Dean Richards those names.

Now that Donna had officially told me about Billy, it was time to do some investigating. I didn't want to pry, but I wanted her to tell me about him. She never brought him up, and I didn't understand why. So I asked around to find out who he was. I wouldn't be a good friend if I didn't make sure he had Donna's best interest at heart.

"Is there a Billy in this class?" I asked the person on either side of me each period. Everyone responded with a no. If he had the same lunch period, Donna would've looked for him, but she never did.

"Daniel," I said before Donna came to the table with her tray. "Do you know a Billy?"

"Billy? Nope. Are you going to eat that?" he asked of my applesauce.

"You can have it."

I was stumped. If I hadn't seen him in Taco Bell with her, I would've thought he didn't really exist. As I sat sipping my juice, it occurred to me that Billy didn't have to attend Stoneburg. He went to another school. Why didn't I think of that at first? That explained it. But then Lisa said, "You mean William? This isn't his lunch period."

I looked over at Donna at the counter and scooted closer to Lisa. "You know him?"

"Not well, but Kennedy does."

Oh, no.

When I wasn't looking for Billy, I was protecting Lisa. Jessica wouldn't let her leave the classroom. Lisa told me she'd acted like she was jokingly holding her back. The teacher fell for it and left the room too.

"I don't want any trouble," said Lisa.

"Too late. Who's going to help you now?" Jessica asked.

"Lisa, are you ready?" I asked from behind her.

"Aria, Dean Richards sent me looking for you, said the girl who ran up to me out of breath.

Jessica gave a wicked grin.

I stepped away from the door and Daniel and Tracey walked into the room. "Let's go, Lisa," said Daniel.

The group from our lunch table and those from the next table looked out for each other. And that now included Denise.

But Kennedy was up to something. She hardly talked to anyone now. It wasn't like her to be so quiet—not the girl who craved everyone's attention. She no longer seemed like a gang leader. At least not until I was in the library and spotted a head of David-Hasselhoff-looking hair. I followed him. A thick hardcover book hid my face as I stood between two rows of books, listening.

"How is it going," Kennedy asked from the other aisle.

"It's going."

She whispered something.

"I'm not comfortable with that," Billy replied.

"Look, Brandon is the one who ratted us out. He's the reason we're all on probation."

How did they think it was Brandon who turned them all in? I thought they blamed Lisa but couldn't get to her because of us. Why him? What had I missed?

"I'm not on probation," Billy replied.

"That's only because no one knows you're involved yet. But you will be if you don't do what I'm telling you."

"What does it have to do with her?"

"She's his friend."

"Then this is revenge?"

"Yes. Look, it's not hard. All you have to do is stop."

"Are you finding what you're looking for?" asked the Librarian.

I ducked and dashed over to her. "This is the fiction section, right?" I backed up where they couldn't see me. "No. You're in nonfiction, sweetie."

"Oops. Thanks." I hurried to the nonfiction aisles and waited for them to leave the library.

Kennedy had ended the conversation by telling Billy, "All you have to do is stop,"

Stop what?

Not long after I'd gotten home from school, the doorbell rang.

"I'll get it!" I set my hot water cornbread on a plate and hurried to the front door. Through the peephole I saw the back of a long black wool coat and earmuffs over shoulder length dark hair.

"Hello?"

She whirled toward me as I opened the door.

"Hey, Aria. I'm dropping off the new brochure." She handed it to me. *She's an Avon lady, going door to door? In the winter? Come on, Aria, think. Do you remember her coming by before?*

"I'm going to Kennedy's next since you guys usually order the same thing. I know you were looking at that necklace with the solid perfume inside."

The pendant. I remembered it. But that was for kids. I only wanted it because it reminded me of my mom. She'd gotten me a similar one when I was little—when we lived in New York. Back then it made me feel like an adult to have my own perfume.

"Did you go inside her house?" I don't know why I thought to ask that. I suddenly remembered no one ever did. You'd have to sit out on her front steps to talk with her.

"No. Come to think of it, they're pretty private. She always comes outside for her order."

"Has she ordered recently?"

"Neither of you have. And I'm sorry about your mom. I took a chance that you might want a little something."

"I'll see if it's okay with my father. Can I call you?"

"Yes. Sure. You have my number. I'll see you later."

I immediately called Donna. "Can you go somewhere?"

"Where?"

"To spy on Kennedy."

"Mom, can you drop me off?" she yelled.

"The Avon lady should've just left," I said as Donna and I walked toward the large ranch-styled red brick home.

We stood behind a tree looking for signs someone was home. "It's a really pretty house," said Donna.

"Yeah, it—"

Donna darted across the street. I couldn't believe she took off like that with no plan. I ran after her, through the neighbor's yard to Kennedy's.

"Look, there's a patio door over there. Stay low," I told her.

"Are the curtains open? They may see us."

"No. Go to that window."

We grabbed onto the brick ledge below the window and lifted ourselves just high enough for our eyes to see over the sill.

There were stacks of things everywhere. Newspapers, magazines, books, furniture.

Beyond it, down the hall, Kennedy walked past, following a woman.

"Is that her mother?" Donna whispered.

"Where did they go? Go that way!" We ran to the next window where we could see better. It was more of the same. Items everywhere in what could've been a family room. Her mother looked behind her and pointed at Kennedy. Kennedy's arms were outstretched as if pleading with her. And then, WHAM! Her mom turned and smacked her. Kennedy fell back against a cabinet and covered her face.

"Did you see that?" asked Donna. I didn't respond, and we didn't take our eyes off the window.

After Kennedy's mother yelled in her face and stormed into the next room, Kennedy lowered her hands from her tear-soaked face and looked toward the window.

Donna and I stood erect, turned to run, and slammed into each other. We fell back on our bottoms, jumped up, and ran along the side of the house. "Which way?" asked Donna.

"Keep going, around the front."

We turned and stopped. Kennedy stood there waiting

NINETEEN

Picture the worst scene from a horror movie. That's what we were in. Kennedy didn't speak. Her arms were pressed in at her sides, her feet planted together. The breeze lifted her Farrah Fawcett curls away from her face. Her eyes were red from crying, with dark rings under them. Her face was etched with anger.

But what was frightening was the grey smoggy mist that rose and looped around her.

Donna stood behind me but moved closer.

"Do you see that?" I whispered.

"See what? Kennedy?"

"Tell them it's all a lie," Kennedy demanded. Her voice didn't raise, but its sternness had the same effect of someone yelling in your face.

She didn't ask what we were doing there or why we were looking through her window. I don't even think she cared about what we saw, as shocking as it was.

Who would believe they were hoarders? There's more to everyone than you actually know. But this—no one would believe.

"I can't do that. I told the truth."

"That's too bad."

That's all she said and walked back inside the house. Donna grabbed my arm and sounded as if she were hyperventilating when she spoke. "I thought she was going to kill us."

"No, not us. We need to find Brandon."

"Where to?" asked Donna's mom as we hopped in. She sat with her thick wavy hair tucked into her coat, looking in the backseat at us.

I loved her. She was down for anything. And probably the adult we shared the most with.

"Where does he live?" asked Donna.

"In this area. He said he lives off Pierce Road."

"That could be anywhere."

"Pierce is just around the corner," her mom replied as she drove. Their station wagon was old, smelly, and the engine ran hard. But Betsy, they called her, got us wherever we needed to go. The funny thing about it was unlike other people, anxious to show off the latest this of that, they could afford a better car; they just didn't want one.

Donna and I looked down each side street as we drove by. "What are the odds he's outside, let alone, us seeing him?"

"I've got an idea," said her mom.

"What are you going to do?"

She stopped in the middle of the street and blew the horn. I ducked.

"Someone is bound to come outside looking. It might be him." She went right on honking.

She was right. Many people came out of their homes, probably wanting to strangle her. "Hey, you two. How are you going to see anyone if you're hiding? Look, is that him? What about the guy yelling from the front door?"

"I'm so embarrassed," said Donna. "It's not him. Mom, please drive."

She pulled onto the next street. "Look," I exclaimed before she could go to blow the horn again. "It's Brandon."

"Mom, pull over!" said Donna.

I hopped out of the car and ran up to him. "Brandon!"

"Hey. What are you doing over here? I'm going to the store to get some Lemonheads. Remember those?"

"Lemonheads? What's wrong with you? *You're* a lemon head. Stop settling into this life." I took a deep breath. "I know why we're here. Will you take the journey even though you know where it leads?"

"Here we go again," he said, walking away.

"No. Listen. A little while ago I saw-I saw… The Murk surrounded Kennedy."

Brandon stopped walking. "So what does that mean? Why are we here?"

"To save…" I almost couldn't say it. "Kennedy."

"You've got to be kidding me. Why would we come back here for Kennedy? This is *my* life. What does my life have to do with her?"

"Life is more than about you. It's bigger than you. You have to save her to save yourself." He started walking again, and I followed. "I thought I could choose who to help but found out it doesn't work that way." I remembered hearing, "There is one greater who knows all and knows who you must help. You are only to follow instructions, even if you feel you hate them. You don't know what their future holds. In judging them, you are no better than they are." I told Brandon—not about the voice, but those very words.

He stopped walking, and I walked into the back of him. "I don't want anything to do with her," he said. "You saved her life once, didn't you? From that downed power line? What good did that do? What happens if we don't?"

"You die."

He was just as shocked as I was to hear the words come from me. I don't know how I knew it, but it was true.

"You're lying," he said and turned on his heels.

"Brandon!"

He ran down the street as if he were running for his life.

Donna walked up to me. "Well, that didn't go well."

"No, it didn't."

"My house?"

"Yeah, I need a drink."

"I know you don't mean liquor because we aren't alchies. You mean fruit punch, right?"

"Yuck. I don't drink anything red."

"Why didn't I know that?"

Donna watched me from across the counter. "I don't know how you can eat at a time like this."

"We have to keep up our strength, don't we?"

"For what?" she laughed.

"I don't know. It sounded good when it popped into my head. What are you listening to?"

She plopped into a huge cowhide recliner rocker. "You don't know who this is? I thought you knew all kinds of music. It's Van Halen."

"I do, but excuse me for failing your test," I said while taking a bite of my sandwich.

"There's something about boys with long hair, right?"

"If you say so. You're especially happy despite what happened today." I exaggerated my stare as if I was examining her—tilting my head left and right in her face. "You're not your normal concerned self. Why? Could it be Billy? What's up with him?"

She averted her eyes. "He's, uh, my boyfriend now."

"He is?"

"Yes. He asked me at the arcade. We talk on the phone almost every night—like for hours."

She was so happy that it made my stomachache. Their relationship was a lie, but I didn't know how to tell her. So instead I said, "Tell me all about him."

TWENTY

Kennedy may have hated Lisa, turned against Brandon, and booted Denise, but all the while, she was setting a trap for her next victim.

Two days later, I saw the results of her plan. Donna was a mess. I'm talking, bloodshot eyes and snot dripping from her nose onto her lips. "He stopped calling two days ago."

"The day we went to Kennedy's?"

"I guess so. He acted like he didn't even know me at school," she cried.

"Tell me this, when did he ever walk the halls with you? Did anyone ever see you two together?"

"No. But that was because we didn't want anyone to know about us."

"If a boy truly cared, it wouldn't matter who knew." My voice softened as I watched her open a quart of ice cream. "Forget him. There will be others. You deserve better."

Donna dropped the ice cream scooper and pointed at her chin. "Look at my face, Aria. How many people do you see walking around with this kind of defect?" Her mouth seemed to twist even more, showing her deformity. "It's not every day that a boy shows me attention."

"That's what they were betting on."

"They?"

"It was all a game. Kennedy put him up to it. They did this to you to hurt the person *I* care about."

"No... They have nothing to do with this."

"Donna, I'm not trying to be cruel, but I have to say this point-blank. Billy never really liked you. And if he did, he wouldn't let them know it."

"That's a lie. You're just jealous. He said you would be. That's why I didn't tell you."

I was about two seconds away from grabbing her shoulders and shaking her. "What did he say? That I wouldn't like anyone else being your friend?"

"That's exactly what he said," she slowly replied.

"Who do you believe?"

I waited, but it took too long for her to respond. "I'll leave you to think about it," I said as I grabbed my coat and left.

It wasn't long before Donna yelled my name out the front door. Then she looked down, seeing I was sitting there on the step. They wanted to break her but didn't count on me being there to pick up the pieces. I hopped up without giving her the opportunity to say anything.

"Dry your eyes. Don't give them the satisfaction."

"Okay," she whimpered.

"I don't think I can watch you dip another one of those Doritos into your vanilla ice cream. Yuck. Why do you do that?"

She tried to smile.

"They're trying to get back at me." I didn't bother to mention Brandon or what I overheard in the library. "It's not about you. Nothing they did bothered you anymore, so they had to find a way. They put him up to it."

She stopped crying and wiped her eyes with her shirt. "I'm sorry I pushed you away when he entered the picture. I know I wasn't calling you much."

"Yeah, you were all in Billy-zone. Billy, Billy, Billy. Ugh. I still love you though."

"I'm never going to have a boyfriend. I'm going to be the girl who has to go to prom with her brother."

"You don't have a brother."

"Then my cousin."

Tear-soaked strands of hair stuck to her face. I pulled some away from her eyes. "Trust me, I've seen the future, you're going to be just fine. With your fluffy bouncing-and-behaving red hair and those eyelashes..." Donna's eyes lit up.

"Everything is falling apart for them. It'll be good for them to see their tricks no longer work. But I need to figure out what they have in store for Brandon."

"Aria," she sniffed. "Have you forgiven yourself for what you almost did?"

"Yes. I think so. Why?"

"I've been thinking. Maybe Brandon must, too."

"That, and there's a monster after him."

"A monster? Why does it want him?"

Donna was the only person who could listen to me say something like that and not flinch. "Because he's not supposed to be here. It's behind the deaths."

"What deaths?"

"Oops..."

"Now look who has secrets."

"Nope. Not the same. The future you knows about it."

"Give me a break. Tell me. What deaths?"

"The deaths of every student who has died at Stoneburg."

"How?"

"The best I can determine is that it's using Mrs.—wait a minute. It's not Mrs. Kohn at all," I whispered. "It's Kennedy. It's using Kennedy to drive them to that point— to suicide."

"I know what it is, then," said Donna.

"What?"

"Pure evil."

"That's about how I'd put it."

TWENTY-ONE

I knocked on Denise's storm door. I hadn't as much as stepped foot on her property in months. Someone wearing a long denim dress looked up and waved me in. She was on the phone. Her house looked to be newly decorated with blue-grey walls and black furniture. Pictures of Denise and her little brother from babies, through grade school, covered the wall behind the sofa.

"I can take a message," Denise's mother said, and wrote something on a piece of paper. "I don't know where that girl is. I thought she was here. Hold on a minute." She set the phone receiver on the glass dining room table and held a finger up to me with a smile.

"Denise," she called down the hall.

I took a step closer to the table and glanced at the note: *Meet me at the clubhouse.*

"Mom, I'm down here," Denise yelled from the basement. "I can't hear you over the washer."

I slowly backed out the front door, making sure the storm door closed softly.

"Where did she go? Aria was just here." I heard her mother say.

"She was?"

A walk to Clio road, a bus ride for her, a cab ride for me, and a trek past downtown. I'd followed Denise, hiding behind cars, mailboxes, and people, fueled by curiosity and an overwhelming desire to save Brandon and get back to my real life.

Denise crossed the street to Stoneburg and went around the side of the main building. *School? She's supposed to be going to the clubhouse.* I waited, watching from the corner, and went to a payphone.

"Donna, I followed her."

"Who?"

"Denise. She's going to their secret clubhouse."

"Why didn't you take me with you? Where is it?"

I looked around the phone booth as Denise disappeared. "Behind Stoneburg?"

"School?"

"I guess so."

"Okay, I'm on the way."

"No, don't bother. I'm just going to see where it is. I'll be home by the time you get here."

"Are you sure?"

"Yes."

"Promise you won't do anything?"

"I'm just going to see where it is."

"Okay."

I ran as fast as I could to catch up to Denise. I'd thought I'd taken too long, having made two calls, but there she was, stepping carefully through the lawn as if she were expecting to fall into a hole.

Where is she going? There is nothing back here.

Behind the next building, a cellar door opened.

Denise walked down the stairs, but she didn't close the doors behind her.

I was out in the open with nothing to shield me. Still, I ducked and scurried over. I peeked in but saw nothing other than cement stairs.

"You came? Are you an idiot?" someone asked.

"I didn't want you threatening my brother," Denise replied.

I stepped down on the first step and waited, and then two more. When I got to the bottom, I strained to hear what was happening on the other side of the door. A few minutes later, it opened. A girl was leaving.

"She's here!" she said—afraid, like this was a western movie and I was going to shoot up the saloon. She backed up.

I stopped there for a moment, not knowing whether to continue in or bolt out of there. *This is what you wanted, Aria,* I told myself. *Time to finish it. You won't fail.*

I took one step into the room. That was enough, so they couldn't close the door behind me.

"Are you okay, Denise?" I asked.

She nodded, standing next to a dirty red velvet loveseat. There were a couple of chairs beside it and a coffee table covered with remnants of chips and other foods, candy wrappers, and soda and beer cans. Someone had sprayed graffiti on all the walls.

About ten students for Stoneburg were down there. Jessica stood to my right with her arms folded over her chest.

"It takes a special kind of bald-eagle-stupid to show up here."

I don't know what happened, but I flinched. I think it was a mosquito. My arm raised and socked Jessica in the eye. She fell back against a rack of boxes. Two kids that were sitting stood as if they were going to do something to me. I mustered up the nastiest look I could give, assuring them I wasn't afraid—that I was 'in charge up in this mug,' as Uncle James would say.

"Get out of here, Aria!" yelled Brandon.

At the far wall, two boys held his arms. Kids I'd never seen. How big was this outfit, anyway?

Calvin held a knife to Brandon's chest.

"Stop! You don't want to do that, Calvin. We can talk about this!" I yelled. I wanted to rush at him, but I didn't want them to close the door behind me, trapping me inside. They might try to surround me.

But Calvin's plan was not to cut him. Brandon's shirt was open at the top. Calvin cut away the buttons one by one while Brandon tried to break free, squirming and sweating profusely.

"Your boyfriend had a plan to burn down the clubhouse. He showed up here with lighter fluid."

Brandon, no.

"They told me they had you down here," Brandon shouted.

Kennedy entered the room from behind them. "Aria, welcome back. It's been a long time since you've come for a visit. Have a seat. Make yourself at home," she said, sounding like a gracious host.

"No. I'll stand."

"Suit yourself." She glanced at Brandon, sighed, and then turned back to me. Something was different about her. When Kennedy didn't like you, she was mean, but here she was wicked. Her hazel eyes were cold and dark. They weren't the eyes of the girl I once called my friend.

"Guess what?" she asked. "I figured out a way we can work everything out." She chuckled, "It's the best. You're going to love it. So you send another letter to the paper telling them you lied. It will solve everything. Mr. Jeffrey and Dean Richards will believe the news report. I mean, don't we all? Then my aunt can get her job back and an apology from the Stoneburg Academy board."

"Or?"

"Or Calvin continues, and I send a letter saying *you* lied, and..." She turned in a circle with her arm outstretched... "I tell them this place is your doing—your clubhouse. You're the leader of the gang. That boombox over there... I remember when you stole that."

"I did not!"

"They won't know that, and everyone in this room will back me up. So what do you say? Do we have a deal?"

"Don't do it, Aria," said Brandon.

Calvin punched him in the stomach. I shrieked and stepped back with my hands covering my mouth.

"Did I get it, I missed it, didn't I?" He asked Brandon while holding his face. Brandon grimaced in pain. The boys holding him were the only thing keeping him upright.

Footsteps came from behind me. "I'll tell them she told the truth," said Lisa.

"Get out of here. You're not welcome anymore. Jessica." Kennedy said.

Jessica turned to her, finally removing her hand from her face, and I stepped away from the door and between them.

"I have letters too," said Lisa. Her voice shook. "And they tell a whole lot more than Aria's did."

"They won't believe you."

Feet bounded down the stairs.

"They'll believe more than one of us," said Daniel.

"That's right," said Denise, coming to my side. "We'll all back her up."

Without turning around, I knew there were more students on the stairs. Well, that and how those in the room looked behind me and seemed unnerved.

"How's Billy?" asked Kennedy with a sly grin. That's when I knew Donna had arrived also.

"Psycho sociopath," said Donna as she stepped beside me.

I placed my hand on her arm, telling her to calm down.

"I have a better idea. This is what you should do…" I walked up to Kennedy until I was directly in front of her face and lowered my voice. "You could tell what's happening to you at home and have your mother arrested."

Her face softened for a moment and then switched to a cold stare.

My eyes shot to Brandon. I looked around the room. We both felt it. I could see it in his eyes. Then I saw the mist rising around Kennedy.

"Brandon! Look at me!"

He did. And so did everyone else.

"Will you—"

"Yes, I'll take the journey." He said with tears in his eyes. "Let's change the memories."

I nodded. "No matter what happens?"

"No matter what happens," he agreed. "Failure isn't an option. Don't let go."

"What kind of foolishness is that?" asked Calvin. "Some kind of Romeo and Juliet speech?"

"Help her," said Brandon.

"Help who?" Kennedy half-laughed and then looked confused when I faced her.

Calvin pointed the knife at Brandon's stomach. "Answer her. Don't make me—"

"Go ahead. I'm not resisting anymore. Cut if off. Show everyone. I don't care."

I heard a commotion behind me and stepped aside.

The man stood well over six feet tall and had to duck a little upon entering. He placed all of his attention on Brandon. "You don't think I care, but I do. You don't think I understand what you're going through, but I don't have to. I feel you as much as my heartbeat. Your joy is mine, as well as your pain."

He spoke as he walked toward them. Calvin and the others looked around like they didn't know what to do. He grabbed Calvin's hand that held the knife and squeezed it so hard, while looking him in the eye, he dropped it.

"How did he get here," Donna whispered.

"I called him before I called you. He said Brandon had gone to some clubhouse."

"Dad," said Brandon.

"Are you going to let him go, or do I have to make you?"

The boys released him and backed away.

"You should be ashamed of yourselves.

"You're responsible for what you do in this life. But also, what you've caused to happen. The hurt and the pain. That's all on you. The wrong you've encouraged them to do, that's on you too," he said, facing Kennedy. "May God have mercy on your soul."

Kennedy looked horrified. She turned and ran down a back corridor to another door. Brandon followed her, yelling her name. Beyond the corridor were stairs. They led up to the main floor of the school.

"Kennedy!"

"No! Stay away from me."

"Brandon!" his dad called.

"I'll get him, sir," I assured him.

Kennedy would not stop running. I think she was trying to escape from everything, including this life.

Up the stairs we ran until we came out on the roof. Large drops of rain and sleet fell over us.

Kennedy stood at the edge, looking over. Brandon approached her. I turned back to those behind me with a finger over my lips and carefully stepped closer to Brandon. But not too close.

"Kennedy, come back inside. It's going to be okay."

She shook her head hard. Her hands were balled into fists and held tight to her mouth as if she were biting them. "No, it's not."

Brandon yelled out, and I fell back as the Murk shot up around her, almost obscuring her from vision. It pulsed and appeared to be solidifying.

"Brandon!" his father's voice came from behind me and I feared he'd interfere.

"It's blocking her off! We have to get to her!" I yelled.

I knew it was using the same mind games it had used on me, on her. Everyone hates you; life is better without you—whatever it needed to say to get her to jump.

She stepped upon the ledge.

"What happened to the others, should have been me the whole time. I'm the one who doesn't want to be here," she said.

Brandon stepped closer and closer as the Murk's force pressed against him. "Kennedy, I won't let you go!"

"Brandon, what are you doing?"

He reached his hand inside and disappeared into the mist. There was a pop, like from an electrical charge. I looked away from them at the trees and followed the drooping wire to the building. *It can't happen. Not again.* "Even if they don't touch each other, if the wires so much as droop onto trees..." My dad had said. I ran to the roof edge and looked over.

It wants both of them.

"Brandon!" I called.

Suddenly, a hard gush of wind blew over us. The wire dropped, touching a corner of the building. There was a sound I don't think I will ever forget. Like a motor revving up. I covered my eyes with my arm from the bright light as it exploded. Screams came from the door of the stairs. Over my elbow, I could see Brandon holding Kennedy.

A wail released from her like nothing I'd ever heard. And with it a roar from the Murk that made me squat and cover my ears for fear my eardrums would explode.

A moment later, I dropped my hands and opened my eyes. The Murk was gone.

Brandon's dad rushed to him.

Donna grabbed me. "Are you okay? You are going to have to explain everything that just happened. What did you guys see that blocked her off?" she asked, eyes wide. "And that explosion... It was almost like that first time you saved her."

"We'll talk later," I whispered.

Brandon still held Kennedy as she cried and hugged me too with one arm when I walked over.

"How did you do it?"

"I told her I would save her, and I wouldn't let go, no matter what."

Just like my angel, I thought.

Brandon's dad wrapped his coat around Kennedy, and we all moved away from the door as he and Brandon walked her downstairs.

"I can't believe you guys came here," I told my misfit crew.

"I had a feeling you needed backup," said Donna. "I called Lisa first, because she lived the closest."

"After everything you've done for me, I had to come," said Lisa.

We walked down the stairs and back through the cellar. Calvin sat on the red sofa staring at the floor. Everyone else had fled.

"We're like vigilantes," said Daniel, once we were outside. "We need a name for a group of people who exact punishment in return for a wrongdoing."

"You mean an avenger. That's the definition of an avenger," said Tracey.

"Then yeah. That's the word for us."

"That's a comic book," said another boy. "You are so out of touch with life."

"That's because he only thinks about computers."

"They're the future," said Daniel.

The future, I thought. What a great way to repay them. "I'm going to give you all a gift for showing up for me."

"Food?" asked Daniel.

"No. Remember this word: Macintosh. Write it down."

"What's it for?"

"Just remember, I told you. Say it ten times."

They all did.

"Now she's got us chanting like Buddhists about apples," Daniel said as police cars pulled up behind Brandon's father's car.

TWENTY-TWO

It was finally over. I felt lighter than I'd ever felt, and happy. I'd even started breakdancing again and tried to teach Donna, although that was a disaster.

What I couldn't figure out was why I was still in 1982. Brandon and I had fixed things. We'd broken the Kohn curse was the way I saw it. It was time to go home.

I tried to make the most of my time and change as much as I could for the younger me and my friends. I wrote a final letter to the newspaper forgiving everyone and met with Dean Richards about implementing a program about bullying.

Mrs. Kohn didn't get her job back, but it was good to know she wasn't the one behind everything like I'd once thought.

Denise and I were working on our friendship again. My dad was at work, and we were sitting in the living room doing homework and watching MTV when the doorbell rang.

"Good googly goop, Riri! Why aren't you ready to go?"

"Go where?"

"Your father told me to be here at six to take you to Mrs. Janice."

The therapist? I do that now? "But it's six-thirty, Uncle James."

"Better late than never."

"Hey, Deedee. What's good?"

Denise gathered her books. "It's Denise. Nothing, Sir. We can finish later, Aria."

"Okay."

As Denise walked out, Brandon walked in.

"Hey, we're just leaving."

"Oh."

"You want to ride, boy?" asked Uncle James.

"Tacos?"

"Yep."

"I'm in."

"Get your coat, girl," said Uncle James.

Brandon smirked. "Yeah, get your coat, Riri."

I walked into a large room with a group of girls sitting in chairs arranged in a circle. Mrs. Janice was there too, my mom's therapist friend.

She pointed at a chair and I sat, suddenly remembering being there before, as if the memories were just added. My dad had insisted that I attend, but I was surprised at who sat across from me. She was in the middle of speaking:

"I once reported what was happening at my house—the abuse. No one believed me, because we were the Kohns. Like local royalty. I've done a lot of bad things. I guess I'm just like them." She looked up, seeing I was there. "I hope the people I hurt can forgive me.

"There are a lot of people I need to apologize to. I pushed them. I made their lives just as miserable as mine. I manipulated them to see what I could get them to do. It was all in fun."

Yeah, but people died, I thought.

"I took things too far. It wasn't that I lacked feelings. Well, maybe I did at times. But I couldn't fix what I'd done. So I pretended I was okay with it. I can keep apologizing, but I know it's not enough. Maybe one day you will forgive me. Maybe God will forgive me."

She believes in God now?

"But that's the easy part. You have to forgive yourself," said a girl beside her, biting her nail.

"Forgiving myself doesn't stop the memories. You can't stop thoughts. They come out of nowhere and I remember every stitch of what I've done. I guess that's my prison."

No one spoke for a while.

"I just tried my best to make it through each night at home. School was where I was free—what I could control. People, I mean."

"Are you saying what you think she wants to hear?" I asked, pointing at the therapist.

Kennedy sat erect. "I'm being honest."

"Aria, please," said Mrs. Janice.

I looked away and flipped my hand at her for her to continue.

"No, I'm done," she said with a sniff.

"Okay, that will end tonight's session. Everyone..."

We all recited the serenity prayer with her: "God grant me the serenity to accept the things I cannot change, courage to change the things I can, and wisdom to know the difference."

We stood and hugged each other. Many of these girls never received hugs other than what they received at those meetings. I watched Kennedy walk to a matronly woman that waited for her at the door. I ran to catch up with her. "Kennedy!"

I slowed, not knowing what I wanted to say. *You made me hate you*, is what I thought. Instead, I hugged her.

"Thank you for coming tonight. I didn't think you would."

"Take care of you. Here..." I tapped her temple, "and here," I placed my palm flat against her chest.

"Thank you, Aria. I will. How is Brandon? Is he okay?"

"Look outside."

She placed her fingers between two slats of blinds and looked out at the parking lot. Brandon waved up at her.

"He forgives you; you know?"

She teared up. I hugged her again, and she left with the woman.

When I walked out of that building, I almost felt if I jumped in the air, I'd take flight. Simply weightless.

"How did it go?" asked Brandon.

"Good. You saw Kennedy in the window, right?"

"Yeah."

"I think she's going to be okay."

"Get it this car," yelled Uncle James. "I've got women to see and things to do."

"Women?" asked Brandon.

"Ignore him.

"One sec, Uncle James."

I lifted my hand for Brandon to shake it.

"You think?"

"Let's find out."

We took our gloves off and clasped hands. Nothing happened. "Looks like our journey isn't over yet."

I almost let go of him, but I felt a small tingle. "Wait."

Everything shifted around us: The air, the cement under our feet, the office building I'd exited, the cars in the parking lot, Uncle James standing with his hands on the roof of the car looking at us, the sky, the trees. All of it swayed, blurred, and then disappeared.

Suddenly, light and swirls of color surrounded us. Blurred images formed and surrounded us on every side.

Brandon and I stared at our hands, looked up into each other's faces, and grinned. We hugged each other. "We're back!"

He placed a hand on either side of my head and screamed into my face. "I'm back!" He let go and jumped around the roof. He teetered toward the edge and almost stumbled over.

I grabbed him and pulled back. "Hey! Watch it!"

"Oops, I'd better be careful." He danced again. I stood there grinning. I knew that feeling. But as soon as you're back, you're also left with the sense that there's something you have to do. He stopped moving. "I need to call my parents."

"Go, do that."

He ran towards the door and turned back. "I guess I'll see you around?"

I nodded. "Yep."

"Thank you, Aria."

I blushed as he went through the door and I turned and looked out over the campus. I guess this was my life now. It left me with an amazing feeling, having helped someone and set some things right.

When I finally got to my room, I noticed a bunk above my bed, but the room was empty. I wasn't surprised. Something had changed every time I came back. It was the middle of the day, but I went to bed. My body was exhausted, as if I hadn't slept in weeks.

I slept long and hard and awoke wiping drool from the side of my mouth. The room was dark except for the light from my alarm clock. I looked around with a grin, glad I was still there. "Yes! 1990. Feels Good," I sang.

"Hmmm..." came from the other twin bed. "I'm sorry, Donna. I didn't mean to wake you."

She turned onto her side, squinting at me, and pushed her braids out of her face. "Why are you calling me Donna?"

I jumped back. "Kennedy?"

Donna looked down over the side of the top bunk. "Why are you calling her Donna?"

Middle to late adolescence is the most common age when symptoms first appear or a first major depressive episode happens (Burke, Burke, Regier, & Rae, 1990). Lewinsohn, Hops, Roberts, Seeley, and Andrews (1993) randomly sampled adolescents within a U.S. community and discovered that the average age of onset of major depression was 14.

*If you suspect that a teenager is suicidal, take immediate action! For 24-hour suicide prevention and support in the U.S., call the National Suicide Prevention Lifeline at **1-800-273-TALK**. To find a suicide helpline outside the U.S., visit IASP or Suicide.org.*

Visit www.IAMARIA.org for further resources and support regarding teen depression. You'll find posts from professionals, parents, and teens, who have dealt with depression and know what you are going through.

Please Leave A Review

Your review means the world to me. I greatly appreciate any kind words. Even one or two sentences go a long way. The number of reviews a book receives greatly improves how well it does on Amazon. Thank you in advance.

Review here:

https://www.amazon.com/dp/B08L5N732Q

Exclusive content, discounts and giveaways
are available only to L. B. Anne's VIP members.
Use the link below to sign up.
There's no charge or obligation.

https://www.lbanne.com/vip-club

The Everfall series introduced you to Gleamers and the Murk. Read L. B. Anne's, Amazon best-selling, Sheena Meyer series to find out more.

THE SHEENA MEYER SERIES

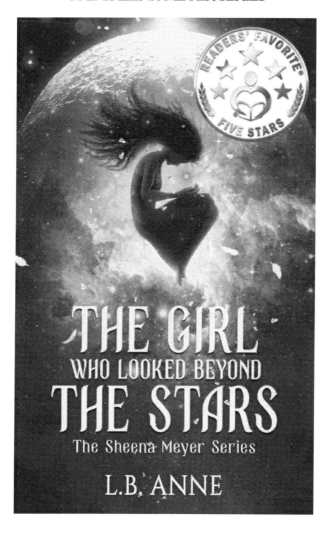

ABOUT THE AUTHOR

L. B. Anne is best known for her Sheena Meyer book series about a girl with a special gift, and a destiny that can save the world. L. B. Anne lives on the Gulf Coast of Florida with her husband and is a full-time author, speaker, and mental health advocate. When she's not inventing new obstacles for her diverse characters to overcome, you can find her reading, playing bass guitar, running on the beach, or downing a mocha iced coffee at a local cafe while dreaming of being your favorite author.

Visit L. B. at www.lbanne.com/home

Facebook: facebook.com/authorlbanne

Instagram: Instagram.com/authorlbanne

Twitter: twitter.com/authorlbanne

Printed in Great Britain
by Amazon

11605341R00114